Consumed
by You

a Fighting Fire novel

Lauren Blakely

Entangled Publishing, LLC
2614 South Timberline Road
Suite 109
Fort Collins, CO 80525
Visit our website at www.entangledpublishing.com.

Brazen is an imprint of Entangled Publishing, LLC. For more information on our titles, visit www.brazenbooks.com.

Edited by Alycia Tornetta and Stacy Abrams
Cover design by Heather Howland
Cover art from iStock

Manufactured in the United States of America

First Edition August 2015

This book is dedicated to all the readers who asked, "What about Travis and Cara?" and to Michelle, Stacy, and Alycia for believing in these books, and as always to my friend Cynthia.

Chapter One

The dress she wore was pure torture.

Red, tight, and snug against every luscious curve of her body, it whispered to him in some kind of smoky, come-hither voice.

Take me off.

Travis would love nothing more than to answer that call, as he watched Cara move like a sensual, catlike creature on the dance floor, in those mile-high heels that had him wishing she were the kind of woman he could take home for the night.

He leaned his hip against the high metal table parked at the edge of the dance floor, enjoying his front row seat to the best view in the house. *Her.*

Cara was temptation herself this evening, her long, silky mane of black hair spilling down her back as those hips swayed in time to the low, pulsing bass that vibrated through the night club. He didn't have a clue how he was going to survive dog training lessons with her later that week, when it was hard enough being this near to her at their friends Smith and Jamie's joint bachelor and bachelorette party.

But, he reasoned, she'd be back to the T-shirt-and-jeans Cara, the hair-in-a-ponytail Cara in a few days, when they started teaching his new Jack Russell mix to sit, stay, and fetch.

That Cara would be easier for him to manage than this temptress, right?

He took a long pull on his beer, finishing it off as he considered his own question. The answer came quickly as he set down the empty bottle. Nah, it wouldn't be any easier. She was just as fucking hot during the day, walking dogs around their hometown of Hidden Oaks, as she was here tonight, dressed for sin in San Francisco.

"How long?"

A hand came down on his back. Travis turned to Smith, who thrust another beer at him. He'd been refilling drinks at the bar.

"How long what?"

Smith nodded to the crew of their friends on the dance floor. "How long before you actually make a move on Cara?"

"Why do you want to know?" Travis asked. No use pretending he hadn't been caught staring.

"Because I'm thinking of getting a pool going at the firehouse. I'm even going to put up a big old poster with squares," Smith said, spreading his arms out wide.

Travis arched an eyebrow, finally managing to pull his gaze away from Cara. "And what will these squares say?"

Smith mimed writing on a whiteboard. "One week from now," he said, tapping an imaginary square on the betting pool. "One year from now." Then another. "Never fucking ever," he said, stabbing his finger into the air. "And that's the one I'm putting my money on."

Travis laughed, talking above the loud music. "Why do you even care if I make a move?"

Smith clutched his chest. "Because it pains me to see a man ogling a woman like that and doing nothing about it."

"Who said I was going to do nothing about it? Maybe I just don't feel like telling you about all the plans I have up here," Travis said, tapping his skull, even though his friend was right—he hadn't been planning on doing a damn thing about Cara. "Plans that would make your betting pool obsolete."

He was bluffing, but he couldn't deny that Smith was onto something. Hell, it pained him, too, not to do a damn thing about this rampant attraction that wound him up like a coiled spring. His focus briefly wandered to the bar where Cara had joined Jamie in a round of shots. Somewhere out on the dance floor, Travis's sister, Megan, was snug up against the fire chief, Becker, while a bunch of their other buddies had grabbed a table in the back. They'd all rented a few limos for the night, riding from Hidden Oaks down to the city so they could fully enjoy the celebration.

Smith shrugged and took a drink of his beer. "My money's on: you're too much of a pussy to do it."

Travis scoffed, his eyebrows shooting into his hairline. "One, I'm not too much of a pussy to make a move on her. Two, why do people use pussy as an insult? I never understood that. Pussy is fucking awesome. It's pretty much the greatest thing in the world. And three, you know she's not interested in a guy like me."

Smith nodded several times and flubbed his lips, as if Travis had just revealed the secrets of the universe. "Yeah, you're right. She probably likes men who actually have the guts to go for her instead of just staring at her wistfully while she's on the dance floor."

Travis rolled his eyes. "That's not what I meant. I would never stare at a woman *wistfully*. When I stare, it's *hungrily*," he said, as he deflected the conversation from the real reason he hadn't acted on his desire for her. Cara was great—she was fun, and sharp, and he'd enjoyed every second of the summer they'd spent together back when they were younger. He could still recall how fiery she'd been between the sheets. But now that they were no longer two horny teenagers screwing in the back of his truck, or two recent college grads reconnecting for one hot night, she didn't have any interest in guys who didn't like settling down. A volunteer firefighter and a professional card player, Travis was not a settler-downer. Hell, he had his sights set on winning the California Bachelor Fireman's Auction in a few weeks—the key word being *bachelor*. So as much as he wanted to have the woman in red again, he was all wrong for her. Even though he wanted her badly.

. . .

"Time for another round!"

Jamie grabbed Cara's arm and practically yanked her off the dance floor. Cara nearly stumbled in her heels from the surprise attack her friend had launched on her elbow.

"Hey! I like that arm. I want to keep it," she said as they made their way to the bar.

"It is indeed a very nice arm. Shapely and toned," Jamie said, patting Cara's bare flesh as they reached the chrome and steel bar at Edge, a nightclub owned by one of Travis's friends.

"So you can see why I'm attached to it," she said, and then her eyes widened as the soon-to-be-bride gestured to a tray with shot glasses and a gorgeous crystal martini glass with a purple concoction.

Cara pointed to the fancy cocktail. "Purple Snow Globe?"

Jamie nodded. "Pick your poison. I ordered a bunch of drinks."

There was no question in her mind. She'd gladly take the sweet, sugary, award-winning cocktail over the burn of a tequila shot anytime. She picked up the drink and clinked glasses with Jamie. "To your wedding."

"I will happily drink to the end of my single days," Jamie said, quickly downing the amber liquid. "Speaking of single days, what are we going to do about you and Travis and the way you two were staring at each other on the dance floor?"

Cara's jaw dropped. "What?"

Holy shit. Had everyone noticed? She thought she'd done a bang-up job sealing away her desire in a Ziploc bag and stuffing it in the back of the freezer. Evidently, she had not. She slapped on her best cool-and-composed look, took a leisurely swallow of her drink, then said, "What are you talking about?"

"Oh, come on," Jamie said, rolling her pretty brown eyes. "The two of you are still checking each other out like you did in high school."

God, it had been so long, and even though she and Travis had flickered back into each other's lives once or twice since, they were never in the same place at the same time for long enough to matter. That hadn't stopped her from wanting him, though.

"Well, that was then. This is now," Cara said, as if she could so easily squash the long-simmering desire she felt for him. She'd try any remedy to get him out of her head. But he was right there, twenty feet away, casually leaning against the side of the table, knocking back a longneck as he chatted with Smith, looking all relaxed and sexy casual.

She did her best to avert her gaze from him, and his dark brown hair, and his piercing blue eyes, and his broad shoulders that were strong enough to carry you, because they were *supposed* to carry you. Just her luck that the already-gorgeous-at-the-time high school football star would turn into one of the hottest firemen in the whole damn world. He'd been branded on her brain and on her body, and the mere handful of men—she could count them on one hand; half a hand technically—she'd been with since then had paled in comparison.

Sigh. What was a woman to do?

"And now is the time to finally do something about it. I see how you're always looking at him at my bar. And God only knows, I practically have to sweep his jaw up from the floor, the way he gawks at you," Jamie said, parking her hands on her hips and staring pointedly. Cara's lips twitched in a faint smile at the confirmation that this attraction wasn't one-sided.

Wait. Why did it matter? She wasn't going to do a damn thing about it. She wasn't into casual hook-ups, and Travis wasn't into serious relationships. Enough said.

"Be that as it may, I'm going to be working with him

the next few weeks, training his new dog. Even if I were to do something about it, it would be foolish," she said, and she didn't intend to let her latent lust rule the day. Besides, she'd managed to resist jumping him since she'd moved back to Hidden Oaks after spending most of her twenties in San Francisco. She could work with the man and his dog, no problem.

Too bad the task was harder tonight, since he'd been giving her what distinctly felt like a good old-fashioned eye-fucking when she'd been dancing a few minutes ago.

"Well, you know what they say about fools," Jamie said, as she flashed a big, bright smile.

Cara shook her head. "No. What do they say?"

"That sometimes the best things in life are the foolish things," Jamie said, rattling off a quote with authority, as if she were reciting poetry in English class.

"I like that," she said, and if they were anyplace but a nightclub with loud music reverberating throughout the cavernous hall, she would have repeated it softly to convey how it made her feel. "Who said that?"

Jamie pointed her thumbs back at herself. "This girl," she said, and both women cracked up.

"All right, you win. You fooled me."

"Let's go see the guys," she said and grabbed Cara's arm once again.

They weaved through tables and bodies, circling behind Smith and Travis, who were chatting it up. As they neared the guys, Jamie tiptoed the final feet and stretched out her hands so she could drop them over Smith's eyes in surprise. But then Jamie stopped short, quickly straightening her spine as she mimed zipping her lips.

Cara froze, and her ears pricked as she keyed in on Smith's voice, saying, "We all know you're hot for Cara and you have been ever since the two of you went to the goddamn prom together years ago. Wouldn't tonight be the night to finally do something about it?"

Cara blinked. Holy shit. She did everything she could to rein in a wild grin at hearing those words—*hot for Cara*. She shouldn't want to hear them so badly. But hell, did they light up her insides. The prospect of the man she wanted so badly doing something about it tonight had her skin sizzling.

Jamie gave Cara a bug-eyed look as she mouthed, *I told you so*. Cara pressed her finger against her lips and continued to listen quietly.

"Why tonight? Because it's your bachelor party?" Travis asked Smith.

"Nope." Smith puffed up his chest and pointed at Travis. "Because I'm going to make you an offer you can't resist. Let's bet right now. Here. You and me. Usual stakes." The tone of the conversation shifted when Cara heard Smith's next words. "I bet you can't even get Cara to kiss you tonight. And there's no way in hell you could ever convince her to go home with you."

Now it was Cara's turn to tug on her friend's arm. She pulled her away from the men and to the epicenter of all important conversations between women at nightclubs—the ladies room. As the door clanged shut behind them, Cara crossed her arms. She wasn't sure if she was mad or turned on.

"I can't believe they just made a bet about me."

"That's what they do."

"Make bets about women?"

"No," Jamie said with a laugh. "They make bets about everything. They're guys. That's just their thing. Personally, I think it's kind of hot that he wants you so much that all his friends can tell."

"You do?"

Jamie nodded and wiggled her eyebrows.

"So what am I supposed to do about it?"

"What do you want to do about it?"

Cara blew out a long stream of air and ran her hand through her dark hair. She wasn't entirely sure at first. A part of her was annoyed to be the object of a bet. But another part of her, the part ruled by her libido, craved the challenge.

Only, she intended to have things her way.

"I'm going to give Travis a taste of his own medicine," Cara said, lifting her chin, ready for the sweet taste of payback.

There was more in play than turning the tables, though. Maybe one final hot, searing kiss with Travis—a kiss for the ages—would get him out of her system.

Chapter Two

She owned the dance floor.

She claimed a spot under the smoky violet lights. The space was crowded, as bodies smashed against bodies, bumping and grinding to the pulsing music, arms high in the air, hands on waists. But she didn't care about them. She didn't focus on anyone else, not her friends somewhere around here, and not all these strangers.

She looked only at Travis, locking eyes with him as a new song began. A risqué number, heavy on the rhythm, with words that were dirty and promised hot nights tangled up together.

Travis leaned against the brushed metal wall, watching her. Jamie had stolen Smith away, so Cara had Travis's focus all to herself, and she savored it. He didn't even pretend he was looking elsewhere. Nope, he stared unabashedly, and his hot gaze thrilled her. Even in the dimly lit club, she was keenly aware of his intense stare, and the way his eyes were fixed only on her.

He'd been undressing her earlier in the evening with those dark blue eyes, and he'd damn near memorized every curve, bend, and twist in her body, it seemed. She might be a pawn in their betting game, but she was a *wanted* pawn, and that gave her power.

Power was fun. Power was intoxicating. Power was a downright aphrodisiac as she glided into a new dance. A private one just for him. Well, if you could call it *private* even though she was dancing seductively in a packed club. But she'd call it that, because this dance was only for him, and it was designed to reel the man in so she could up the ante on their game.

First, she teased him with a slow grind of the hips. Circling. Simulating. Making sure his mind was on only one thing. She swore his fingers gripped the beer bottle tighter as he stared at her like a hunter.

Then, she went for a sensual thrust of her pelvis, a move that would have him picturing a horizontal dance oh-so-clearly now. Judging from the way his chest rose and fell quickly, his mind was fixed on that image.

Next, she ran her hand through her hair, a slow, sensuous touch of her own body.

Her eyes wandered briefly away from his, roaming down his body, and yup, there it was. The hard evidence that her dance was working. He was turned on something fierce.

She went for the pièce de résistance. The move that brought a man to his knees. She brushed her hand down the front of her dress, sliding slowly over her breasts, spreading her fingers across her belly and finally running her palm along her thighs.

Cha-ching.

He set his beer on the table and stalked over to her, his broad chest looking so touchable in his pullover shirt, which was stretched tight across his muscles, and those jeans that fit him like a glove.

"You look like you could use a dance partner," he said, his sexy voice washing over her. The volume of the music was her wing woman. He had to lean in close so she could hear him. He was inches away, and the air between them vibrated with the frequency of desire.

"What makes you say that?"

He jutted up a shoulder. "Call it a hunch. Am I right?"

She tilted her head and bit her lip as she gyrated. He nodded at her, his eyes straying to her hips. "That's what I'm talking about."

She arched an eyebrow. "Maybe I *could* use a dance partner, then. But only if he can handle me."

"Oh, he most definitely can handle you."

"I'd like to see the proof of that," she said, as her heart beat faster and her skin heated up from their flirtation.

"Would you, now?" he said, dropping his hand to her hip, making contact for the first time in years. Her breath hitched from that barest touch, from strong fingers curving into her body, digging into her hipbones, just the way she liked it. His thumb drew lazy circles on the fabric of her dress, and she wanted to thank the universe and curse it, too, because his touch felt so fucking good.

Damn this man.

Then curses went to praise when he fingered a strand of her hair with his other hand. A rush of tingles spread from her chest to her belly, and all that power she stood proud on moments ago drained away in a heartbeat as he pulled her in close. She was no longer the one calling the shots. He was, and he tugged her against him, aligning her body with his strong and very hard—incredibly hard—frame. Then, somehow they started dancing together. But this was no cotillion style or debutante ball dance. This was two bodies slowly grinding against each other. This was the dance of foreplay, a torturous tease of her swaying hips, and his erection pressed against her waist, and the heat inside her shooting sky high.

It was a promise of the kind of night she'd have if she went home with him.

But then she laughed inside because they'd never been one for homes. They hadn't done it in a bed once when they were first together, and that was one of the very many reasons he'd ruined her for other men. Because he'd shown her what wild meant when she was merely eighteen. She was crazy for him then—what eighteen-year-old doesn't fall hard for her summer boyfriend?—and she'd gladly handed Travis her V-card. Okay, maybe it wasn't technically the first time she'd had sex with him that had rocked her world, but her second and third time with him had been spectacular, along with the fourth, fifth, sixth, and so on, as they explored all the hidden spots in their hometown.

While they'd fallen back into each other a few times over the years since, their nights together had never amounted to more. But tonight, my God, it felt like anything could happen, and *everything* should happen. Maybe that's what years of longing could do to a woman. She tried to concentrate on her mission—turning the tables on him, putting one over on the guys and their bet. But that motivation was growing muted and fuzzy as their bodies collided and he dropped his forehead against hers.

"I've been thinking about you all night," he whispered hotly.

"What have you been thinking?" she asked, the breathiness in her voice betraying how damn much she wanted him.

He didn't answer right away. In the span of his silence, she imagined he'd give her a sweet line, because even when they were younger, he was a talker in moments like this, always telling her she was hot, he loved touching her, that sort of thing. But it was no rote compliment that fell from his lips.

His answer was simple.

"Red."

"Red what?"

"I've been wondering if red was a theme for you tonight. If it extended across your entire wardrobe."

She trembled, turning into putty in his hands at the implication. Damn, a few enticing words, and she was ready to launch herself at him. "You have some very interesting thoughts, Travis."

"Oh, you don't even know the half of it," he said in a husky voice, low in her ear, the words sending a burst of tingles down her spine, settling between her legs in a sweet ache.

"Well, you were standing there drinking beer and thinking about my clothes. That's a little odd," she said, teasing him.

He yanked her body harder against him. "Did I say I was thinking about your clothes?" He wrenched back to look her in the eyes. His were full of dark intent, as if his filthy thoughts were written on them for her to read. He dipped his head to her neck, his warm breath on her bare skin. She shivered from the closeness, from the connection.

"Then tell me what you were thinking about," she said.

"All I could do was imagine what you had on underneath this dress," he said, fingering the slim strap on her shoulder. "And if that was red, too. If you were going to let me find out."

"What color do you think I have on?"

His hand traveled down her back on a path to her ass. She gasped as his fingers mapped a slow, tantalizing trail against the fabric of her dress. The man hadn't even kissed her yet, and she was melting. "I know you like color. I know you like changing up the color of your hair. I know you used to make sure your bra and panties matched your outfit," he said, and fine, this was only about sex, but she liked that he remembered that little detail about her. His hand dropped lower, palming her rear. His touch ignited a round of fireworks in her body, a bright pop in her brain. "You'd wear a yellow tank top, and I'd strip your clothes off at the river and find these hot little yellow panties with a daisy flower on the front. Or you'd tackle me in the back of my truck, all in black, with a little lacy black thong on."

She remembered all those times perfectly, too. They were imprinted in her brain.

"I tackled you?"

"You tackled me. I tackled you. It was all good," he said, tripping down memory lane.

"It was. It was all good," she said, intoxicated from his words now, as well as his touch.

"I bet it still would be good," he said, his lips buzzing across her neck, up the column of her throat, until he reached her earlobe.

Oh God, she was cooked. Well past roasting. He could have her any way he wanted, and she was a fool for thinking she could stop at a mere kiss. He hadn't even put his damn lips to hers, and she was ready to climb him like a tree.

No point waiting.

"Please kiss me," she said, half desperate, half commanding. To hell with her plan to work him up and leave him on the dance floor. *She* was the one hot and bothered.

• • •

Screw bets.

The deal with Smith was the farthest thing from his mind. He didn't care one bit about what they'd gambled for—washing the other guy's car in front of the firehouse. Table stakes, but that was their currency, and none of that mattered now. The only thought that occupied his brain was her, and that was pretty much all that had been in his head the entire night. Now, here she was, asking to be kissed. All of his reasons for resisting her had vanished with the feel of her soft curves under his hand, and the shivers that ran through her body when he touched her. Everything that had held him back disappeared entirely in her request.

Though this wouldn't be their first kiss, it would be the first time he touched her since that one night after they'd graduated from college. He wanted this time to be different. Hotter, dirtier, more irresistible. So, instead of heeding her request, he spun her around, so her back was snug to his chest. She leaned into him, letting her soft, silky hair spill down the front of his shirt. That hair was so damn alluring. Perfect for pulling, twisting, even pinning her in place. He grabbed hard on her hips, tugging her delicious ass against his hard-on.

"I've been like this all night for you. But then, that shouldn't be a surprise. Sometimes just seeing you around town turns me on," he whispered in her ear, his words causing a sexy gasp to escape from her lips.

She dropped her hands on top of his, holding on as he ran them up and down the curves of her body. He pressed his lips lightly to her shoulder, leaving a kiss by the strap of her red dress. He continued to move with her, still dancing a slow, torturous, sensual dance. She stretched out her neck to the side, inviting more kisses. He worked his way up, leaving no stretch of her delicious skin unkissed. She pushed back against him, little sighs and murmurs falling from her mouth. He could only imagine what she'd sound like if he took her home right now and had his way with her.

She grasped his hands tighter, threading her fingers through his and squeezing, as if she had to hold on for dear fucking life. Perfect. This was how he wanted her. This was the woman he couldn't get out of his mind. He turned her around in his arms, and she molded her body to his, her hands shooting up into his hair as he cupped her cheeks. He gazed hungrily into her gorgeous blue eyes, so ready to kiss her at last. He dipped his mouth to hers, and the temperature in him shot to the moon. Her lips were sinful and sweet. They wasted no time with slow or lingering starter kisses. They went for it. Pent up, needy, and ravenous kisses. God, she tasted fantastic, and she responded like a dream, aligning her body along his, her breasts pressed against his chest, her sexy hips grinding against his cock.

He kissed her hard, running his hands through her hair,

his fingers curling around the back of her head. He couldn't fathom stopping at a kiss, and certainly not this kind of kiss, which felt like the prelude to fucking. Their tongues swirled, their mouths devoured each other, their breath mingled. And somehow, the distance between them was reduced to nothing.

The pressure in his bones increased. The need to have her multiplied. His body was a tight, hard line of desire, and he *needed* to know what she had on under that dress. He broke the kiss, grabbed her hand, and tugged her off the dance floor, quickly cutting a path through the crowd, around the corner, and down a hallway to a quiet corner of the club. He knew this place; his buddy owned it. And while this might not be a private room, it was a hell of a lot quieter than the dance floor. They were all alone. He backed her against the wall and ran his fingers along her ass. The look in her eyes was wanton and lustful. It was as if she'd entered some other zone, and it made his entire body buzz.

"So, are they red?"

"Find out," she said in the sexiest murmur he'd ever heard in his whole life.

His fingers quickly found their way to the promised land, sliding along the outside of her panties, which were so slick with her arousal that his brain was scrambled. His nervous system was electrified. She breathed out hard, as he pushed up the skirt of her dress all the way to find she was wearing an absolutely enticing pair of white lacy panties.

He groaned appreciatively as he stroked one finger along the fabric that hugged her in the place he wanted to be. Lucky panties. What a lucky piece of lace to spend the night so nice and snug against her beautiful pussy.

"That answers one thing. The other thing I want to know is how much you liked dancing for me, because I fucking loved that tease you were doing on the dance floor."

"You can find the answer to that easily, too," she said, her voice an invitation that he was RSVPing to as he dipped his fingers inside the band of her underwear.

The heat of her sweet pussy became the center of his world. He ran his fingers across her slick flesh. She arched into him, moaning.

"I guess you like dancing for me," he said, his bones buzzing as she rocked into his hand.

"Love it," she said on a pant, barely able to speak.

He moved his fingers faster, exploring all that delicious wetness. "You know I can't stop at kissing you, Cara. Never been able to. Once I touch you, I want all of you," he said, as his finger visited her swollen clit. She cried out, and her eyes squeezed shut. She rocked her hips into his hand, her body seeking out friction, seeking out pleasure.

"Same here," she murmured.

"You're too hard to resist. You've got to know that," he said, his own desire heating to supernova levels as she rode his hand. She was so close and he couldn't wait to take her to the brink and send her flying, then, to find a private room, and to find it stat. He had to be inside her. Had to feel her heat gripping his dick. He circled her clit faster, and she arched into him, her back jammed against the wall, her body under his control. "Oh God, please, I'm almost there, make me come."

"Anytime," he whispered, and thrust a finger inside her, her slick walls clenching around him as he crooked his finger to hit that spot that sent her soaring. She moaned his name, bucked against him, and grabbed his shoulders to hold on. She dropped her face to his chest, biting down hard on his shirt, breaking skin. She muffled her cries while she came undone on his hand.

Like a fucking vision of passion, heat, and unbridled lust.

Soon, she wrapped her arms around his neck, nuzzling against him, layering sweet, soft kisses along his jaw. Those kisses had his heart beating even faster. He was damn glad he'd taken that bet, and he didn't give a shit about the stakes. All that mattered was how she felt in his arms, and the way the afterglow radiated across her beautiful face.

"Cara, do you want to go upstairs? Someplace private?"

She pulled away, looked up at him with those hazy, dreamy eyes. She seemed to be considering his question, and her lips curved up in a grin that made him sure he was going to be spending the evening where he wanted—between those gorgeous legs.

But then, she moved her mouth to his ear and whispered, "No. And I bet you can't figure out why I'm leaving you like this in the hallway."

She let go of him, her arms falling to her side, and her smile a daredevil one. He furrowed his brow. "What do you mean?"

"Oh, I *bet* you know," she said, and then she walked away.

Chapter Three

Pilates at dawn. A few minutes of yoga after her first appointment. An hour on the elliptical during a mid-day break back at her house a few blocks off the town square.

Cara was almost willing to try meditation, but that be-calm-and-zen approach never worked for her. She wasn't prone to relaxation, and she definitely wasn't mellow enough to meditate. She gripped the handles of the elliptical machine in her guest bedroom, zeroed in on the TV screen, and rolled her eyes in delight along with Giada on the Food Network as the hostess bit into another delicious piece of food.

Maybe tonight she'd try that new pasta primavera recipe that Giada had raved about in today's episode. Invite Jamie, Megan, and Kaitlyn over for a girls' night in. No men allowed.

From the moment she'd let the doors to the club fall shut behind her and hailed a cab to take her on an hour-long drive back to Hidden Oaks, she'd done her best to steer her brain onto a new path, as if she could reroute all her neural pathways. Once at home and in bed, she'd reread her favorite passages from *Inside of a Dog*, figuring that would keep her mind trained on other matters. Like how pissed off her body was for not taking Travis up on his offer. Her leave-him-in-the-lurch plan had done nothing to eradicate him from her brain. How could it? Travis had shown yet again why he was the yardstick by which she measured every other guy. She didn't know if the man had some kind of magic touch or if it was simply that the two of them together were combustible, a fiery combination of heat and desire that ignited whenever they collided.

As the closing credits of the TV show rolled, she reached for the remote on the dashboard of her elliptical machine and turned off the cable. She hopped off the machine, her heart beating hard from the workout, and headed down the hallway, where she was greeted by her black and white lab-border collie mix, who'd been taking a dog nap while she worked out.

Violet wagged her tail and lifted her chin for petting. Cara happily obliged, then grabbed her phone to check her afternoon agenda. She'd already logged two training sessions this morning, one with a nervous terrier in a nearby town and his equally nervous owner, and another with the coffee shop proprietor and her stubborn min pin who'd proven to be quite a handful. She had a free hour that afternoon, and then she was leading her advanced training class for dog agility later today.

Since she had a break before her next client, she decided to reward her four-legged best friend. After a fast shower, she yanked her hair into a simple ponytail, then tugged on shorts, a tank top, and sneakers, and walked to the neighborhood park with an off-leash section.

Along the way, Cara tossed a tennis ball up and down in her hand, which made Violet heel even more perfectly by her side, since the pooch was craving that green ball. "At least one of us can get what she wants," Cara said to her dog. Sometimes she liked to pretend that Violet understood her, as she shared her thoughts about life, liberty, and the pursuit of happiness—and oftentimes about the pursuit of love.

That had been a challenging one lately, though her friend Kaitlyn mentioned a few days ago that she had a new guy she wanted to set her up with. His name was Joe, he built furniture, loved dogs, and was an avid hiker. Like her, he was eager to settle down. "Joe's not a play-the-field type of guy. He's handsome and he's ready for Ms. Right, so naturally I thought of you," Kaitlyn had said when she set up the date. Sounded good to Cara, so she'd be seeing him later that week for dinner.

She pushed her sunglasses against the bridge of her nose as the hot June sun of a Wine Country summer beat down on her, warming her bare skin. The weather was one of the many reasons she'd moved back to Hidden Oaks a year ago, since the temperatures here were much more pleasant than in the City by the Bay. Living in San Francisco for the last several years was akin to residing in a wind tunnel. The other reason she'd returned home was her family. Cara was the youngest of three girls by many years, though she was decidedly not an "oops" baby. Her parents adopted her when she was born to a teenage mom, and they gave her as much love and affection as they did her two older sisters. Now she simply wanted to be able to spend as much time with her family as she could, especially since her sister Stacy, who lived in town, was due to have her second child soon. Her parents were in South Carolina for a few weeks, visiting her other sister, Sofie, whose husband's company had sent him there for a year.

So it had made sense to relocate her training business here and start building it locally. There was no other place where she wanted to put down roots.

As she neared the park, her dog began to pick up the pace, ready to chase balls. Such a simple but satisfying activity, and that's what made it rewarding for the both of them. Cara unhooked Violet from her leather leash and tossed her the ball.

Soon, the rote action and the dog's eager response settled her overactive mind, veering it away from that too-sexy fireman for a moment. At some point, she'd have to woman up and let him know why she'd walked off. But since he hadn't chased her down, or even called, she was in no rush to clear the air.

Besides, she didn't know what to say.

Violet scampered to her for probably the hundredth time, her tongue lolling out of her mouth as she dropped the ball at her feet, panting hard and ready for more. As Cara chucked the ball across the wide expanse of green grass in this quiet patch of the park, a flurry of white and brown fur rushed past her, like a sports car racing down the highway. Violet had an accomplice in play. And oh holy hell, Cara's dog recognition radar went off. Violet's new canine playmate belonged to none other than the perpetrator of last night's epic, toe-curling, star-seeing orgasm.

She gulped. Womaning up might be happening sooner

than she expected. Damn small town.

"Come, Violet!" Cara called, even though her dog no longer needed the command to return to her. Even so, Cara rewarded her with praise when Violet arrived at her side.

She steeled herself, taking a deep, fueling breath and turning around when she heard footsteps. Her heart beat faster just from the sight of him. Travis walked toward her, wearing jeans, a white T-shirt, and an unreadable expression—unreadable because he wore dark sunglasses—as he called out to his dog in an exasperated tone.

"Henry, c'mon boy. Come on back."

In a corner of the park, Henry was preoccupied with chasing a squirrel that had hightailed it up a tree. Travis's dog leapt in the air over and over again, looking a bit like a circus performer on his tiny little legs.

"C'mon Henry," Travis tried again, then muttered, "He's been like this all morning. He's not listening."

Cara glanced at him as she threw the ball to Violet, who shot off like a rocket to chase it. "You have to give him a reason to come back to you."

"Oh," he said, arching an eyebrow. "Is that how it's done?"

She nodded, glad to be able to answer his question about dogs, a subject she was well-versed in, and much more comfortable discussing without getting hot and bothered and ready to jump him. "Yes. Give him something he wants."

"What do you think he wants?" Travis asked, cocking his head to the side as he gestured to his dog, who was fixated on reaching the squirrel high up on a branch.

"A treat perhaps. Or some affection," she answered.

"So that's your strategy?"

"Yes."

His lips quirked up. "Did you use that last night with me?"

She rolled her eyes and laughed when she realized she'd walked right into the flirty trap he'd been setting. "No."

He shot her a look that said he didn't believe her. "I'm not sure I agree with you. You gave me a whole lot of reasons to come back." He turned to the dog once more and tried again. "Henry, come."

The dog ignored him, yapping at the tree trunk.

"Let's get your dog." She clapped her hands, then shouted, "Violet, come," even though her dog was already on the return path. When her mutt arrived at her heels, parking herself in a proper sit, Cara called Henry's name next, and the little dog glanced in her direction as she reached into a plastic bag full of small dog treats. She held one up and handed it to Violet as a reward.

Food in the mouth—that's what Henry saw happening, and it was enough to send him into motion.

He took off running, barreling across the grass, and skidding at her feet. Cara fed him a treat then patted him on the head. "Good dog, Henry. You're such a good little boy."

She turned to Travis. "See? We're getting ahead of ourselves in the lesson department, but all you have to do is give him some positive reinforcement when he does what you want."

Travis nodded a few times, as if she made all the sense in the world. She loved making quick progress with dog and owner. "Positive reinforcement," he repeated. "That makes sense."

He kneeled and petted his dog, telling him he was good. When he stood up, he tugged off his sunglasses and looked her square in the eyes. "But I'm confused on something else, so maybe you can explain your training methods with me. You see, I got a hell of a lot of positive reinforcement last night when you cried out my name and left bite marks on my shoulder from coming so hard. But then you took off."

Cara narrowed her eyes and parked her hands on her hips. "Perhaps that's because I'm not a dog."

Chapter Four

He gave her a look that said *you've got to be kidding me.* He couldn't believe she thought that was what he meant.

"Obviously," he said, undeterred. "And I like dogs a hell of a lot. But I like you even more, and I loved touching you, so I can't figure out, for the life of me, why you'd leave like that."

He didn't break his gaze. He kept his eyes fixed on her, and even though he meant every bit of his compliment, he still wanted to know why she took off.

"Really? You really can't figure it out?" she said sharply. He shook his head. "No. Tell me."

"Travis, I heard that bet about getting me to kiss you," she said, as she threw the ball for Violet and both dogs chased after it. "Dogs often learn fastest from other dogs, so Violet can help train Henry," she said, returning briefly to her teacherly tone.

He nodded but stayed firmly on topic. "I figured out that

you overheard, thanks to that that nice walk-off line. Which, by the way, was pretty impressive as far as walk-off lines go, so I have to give you props for that."

She scoffed. "I'm not looking for props for delivering zingers."

He laughed briefly. "That's not what I'm getting at. What I don't understand is why you would leave when we were having a good time."

"If you wanted to know so badly, why didn't you call me?"

He nodded and held out his hand, acknowledging she had a valid point. Still, he had his reasons. "Because you made it pretty clear you weren't going home with me, and I wanted to respect your wishes. I wanted to give you the space you asked for. See? I'm not such a bad guy."

"Travis," she said, her tone softening. "I don't think you're a bad guy. That's not what this is about."

"Then what is it about?"

"Too many things," she said with a heavy sigh, as Violet returned with the object of her affections—a slobbered-on green ball. As she bent down to pluck it from the ground, a dog biscuit spilled from her pocket. Henry pounced on it, like a hawk, gobbling it up.

She shook her finger at him. "No," she said in a firm voice, and he whimpered and backed away.

"He's a bit of a biscuit bandit," Travis said.

"Most of them are, especially when the biscuits have peanut butter in them. Virtually no dog ever, throughout history, has been able to resist peanut butter," she said, and then returned to the matter at hand. "Anyway, to answer your question. First, it's about the fact that just because you got me off in the hallway doesn't mean I want to spend the night with you when I'm the object of a bet. I mean, did you honestly think that would make me want to stay?" she asked as she raised her arm to throw.

He swallowed, and then scratched his chin. Honestly, he had thought that. Why on earth would he think anything else, given how she responded, writhing in his arms, clutching his shoulders, thrusting her hips into his hands? "Cara, the bet wasn't a bad thing," he said, because to him bets were good things. After paying his way through college by playing professional poker, he'd turned himself into a poker expert, teaching Silicon Valley venture capitalists and San Francisco's high rollers how to play better and win bigger by being smarter. It was far more lucrative to make a living that way than it was to gamble away your savings. Even so, he couldn't resist the siren call of a bet, especially since it had been about her. "Look, Smith made it because he knows I still think you're the hottest woman I've ever known. Ever since you came back last year, I can't get you out of my head. Sometimes a man needs his friends to give him a kick in the ass and get him moving," he said, choosing deliberate honesty with Cara. If she was pissed about a bet that made him seem less than forthright, the least he could do now was to serve up the full truth.

Her mouth fell open as he spoke, and her arm was frozen in place. He took that as a sign to continue. "I meant everything I said to you last night. I have wanted you for so long, and I resist you every day when you come by Becker's bar, or when I see you walking around town, or here at the park, and all Smith did was call me on it. And he called me on it in a way that he knew I would respond to. Besides, I thought you had a good time last night," he said softly, as she relinquished her hold on the ball, both pooches careening after it.

"You know I had a great time," she said, and her voice was gentler now. The irritation seemed stripped from her tone. "But you guys set me up, so I wanted to give you a taste of your own medicine. To let you know not to toy with me. Maybe it was all fun and games, and boys being boys, and that's fine on some level. But I'm not a woman who likes being toyed with. Especially because I am ridiculously attracted to you," she said, meeting his gaze straight on.

A wicked grin spread across his face. Pride suffused him. Some part of him knew that he was better off leaving her alone, given all the reasons why the two of them would never work out. But when a man hears those words from the woman he longs for, they have a way of slamming the door on the frontal lobe of his brain and giving the libido free rein. He stepped closer to her and lowered his voice. "Then let's finish what we started."

She squeezed her eyes shut, as if the conversation pained her. When she opened them, she let out a long and frustrated breath then wrapped her fingers around his arm. Damn, the feel of her hand on his muscles turned him on. Every little touch from her was like kindling a fire.

"Because it's not that simple for me. On the one hand, I'm incredibly attracted to you, and I want to bang you six ways to Sunday," she began and his eyes nearly popped out of his head as his dick rose to full attention. "But on the other hand, I know that nothing more than sex will ever happen between the two of us. There's no point in pretending it would ever be anything more, because we both want different things in life. If I let you in again, it won't be good for me."

She tossed the ball once more to the pair of dogs, and they jetted after it.

"I could make it good for you," he said, closing the space between them so he could smell her, all fresh and showery clean. She didn't have on an ounce of makeup, and her hair was swept up in a loose ponytail. But she was as alluring to him now under the midday sun, as she was in the laser lights of the nightclub. "I can make sure absolutely everything is good for you."

She bit her lip and shook her head. "I want that. I want that so much. But the sooner I stop thinking about you, and daydreaming about the sex we've had, and imagining all the things you'd do to me, the better off I'll be," she said. His skin sizzled at first, then cooled off, doused by the cold water of "the better off I'll be." "And honestly, Travis, that's the real reason I walked away last night. Sure, there was a part of me that was irritated, but I'm a big girl. I understand where the bet came from. But if I let myself just fall into bed with you again, it will be so much harder for me to ever have what I want in life. I want what my sisters have. Maybe that makes me sound like a 'typical girl,' but I'm okay with that, because they're both incredibly happy with their families, and so are my parents. That's all I've known, and all I want, and I promised myself I'd be in a position to truly have that by the time I'm thirty." She glanced at her watch and tapped it, then shot him a small smile. "Clock's ticking. So I think we really should just stick to the plan to work together with Henry once a week starting on Monday. If you're uncomfortable with training a dog with me, I can arrange for one of the other trainers I work with to fill in for me. Would you like that?"

He shook his head vehemently. The idea of that rankled him. "I only want you."

"Then I will see you in a few days, and we'll work with your dog," she said, brushing one palm against the other as she sealed up their conversation and shoved last night into a drawer she seemed to have no interest in reopening. She called Violet over, and Henry trotted alongside her. She petted Henry on the head, then said good-bye to both of them. As she walked away, her dark hair bouncing in that ponytail, her stride purposeful, he ran through a hundred compliments he could give her, one thousand ways he could touch her to try to convince her.

But deep down he knew that wasn't what she wanted.

She wanted more than he could ever give, and he had to admit he admired the hell out of her for sticking to her guns. She had a roadmap, and she was dedicated to following it. He was the same way. After his father died in the line of duty when he was only ten, he watched his mother unravel for years, battling depression, struggling with loneliness, and spending all her days missing a ghost. Finally, she healed and met the man she remarried, but those lost years had left their mark on Travis. They were indelibly etched on his heart as a warning. They'd shown him the stark damage that love could do, and the devastation that commitment can wreak on a person when it's stolen from under you.

He never wanted to get close enough to someone to give her the power to crush his heart.

Chapter Five

"So that's why I always loved that movie."

Cara furrowed her brow. She was about to ask, "What movie?" then clamped her lips shut when she realized she'd be revealing that she hadn't heard a word Joe had said for the last few minutes. Instead, she stabbed her fork enthusiastically at a piece of romaine in her Caesar salad and smiled. "Absolutely. I feel the same."

He crinkled his nose. "Really? I don't meet a lot of women who love *Full Metal Jacket*, especially *that* scene with the drill sergeant."

Oh shoot. Was that what he'd been waxing on about? Well, thank heavens she'd tuned it out because he was spot on. There was no love lost between Cara and violent scenes in films. They weren't her cup of tea at all. Give her a comedy with some slapstick humor, or a good old-fashioned spy movie any day. However, she couldn't let on that she had been drifting off, her damn thoughts stuck like an old record on repeat, playing *Ever since you came back last year, I can't get you out of my head.*

"No, it's great. Love that movie," she said, widening her eyes and feigning excitement as she speared a crouton.

"We should go see it, then. There's a showing at a theater in San Francisco in a few weeks. Part of a Kubrik retrospective," Joe said as he held up his fork to dive into his steak. A sandy blond, with green eyes and a trim build, Joe was as nice and as sweet as they came. So Cara slapped on her blinders and gave her full attention to the man across the table from her at the bistro in Sonoma, where they were having dinner courtesy of Kaitlyn's matchmaking.

"Tell me more about the furniture you build, Joe. Are you like Magic Mike?" she asked, as she attempted to reclaim the conversation from the flotsam and jetsam of her driftwood brain.

"You mean am I a stripper?" he asked, shooting her a quizzical look.

"Magic Mike was stripping to try to support his dream to make custom furniture," she explained.

He winked. "Gotcha. So did you want to see me strip?" He wiggled his eyebrows. "Because I'm happy to call for the check if you do."

Her cheeks flushed red. She quickly tried to redirect their chatter again. "That's okay. I'm pretty hungry," she said, digging her fork into her salad for another bite, as if to prove her famished point.

"Do you want to work up an appetite first, before I strip?"

She set down her fork and shot him a sharp glare. Enough was enough. "I was only teasing."

"I know," he said softly, a note of contrition in his tone.

"I'm sorry. So was I. I would never think you'd want a striptease on a first date. Kaitlyn said you had a great sense of humor so I was playing along, and I pushed it too far."

Her shoulders sank. Now she was the heel. She waved a hand as if she could rid them both of the awkward detour. "Don't apologize. I started a lame joke. Anyway, I'm glad Kaitlyn connected us. I'm having a nice time chatting with you."

She flashed a smile. *Fake it 'til you make it,* she told herself. Joe was great. Truly great. He deserved her A game.

"Me, too. You're fun and pretty and I'm enjoying getting to know you," he said, as he clasped his hand over hers on the table. It felt…nice. Warm. Pleasant.

Once they got past the first-date jitters, Joe really did have a good sense of humor. She had to give him some points for going along with her goofy comments. He was brimming with potential. She simply had to zero in on the present, not on the memories of the other night that still spun wildly in the front of her mind, zipping through her bloodstream on a hot trail of desire.

"Tell me more about you, Cara," he said.

I'm almost thirty, I like dancing, both alone and with others, and I sing off-key in the shower, especially to Taylor Swift, Jane Black, and old Madonna tunes. I like to cook, to exercise, to volunteer at the local dog shelter, and my greatest joy lies in teaching animals to have better relationships with the people they live with.

Oh, and there's one more teeny, tiny thing you need to know about me. It's my Achilles' heel when it comes to my stalled romantic life. Did I happen to mention that I'm hung up on someone else, and I simply can't get him out of my system?

Later, Joe walked her to her car and opened the door. "I'd love to see you again, Cara. From what Kaitlyn told me, you and I are very similar and want a lot of the same things in life. I've got some business travel for a conference coming up, but would it be all right if I called you when I return?"

Damn. He was polite, too.

"Of course," she said. Maybe by then, she wouldn't be thinking about that other man. Maybe by then, she could give Joe a chance for real. He had so much promise, and by all measures, he seemed a perfect fit for Cara's plans for her heart.

• • •

Henry wagged his tail and sat perfectly at Travis's mother's feet, his mouth hanging open, waiting for something delicious to drop into it, like a piece of a hot dog or hamburger that Robert was grilling on the porch.

"Mom, have you been giving Henry treats when you watch him?" Travis asked as he dropped off his dog for the next twenty-four hours that he'd be on shift. If it weren't for his mom's offer to take care of Henry while he worked at the firehouse, Travis would never have been able to adopt the dog in the first place. A few months ago, when he'd stopped by to repair a broken pipe under the sink, he'd mentioned offhand that he'd love to get a dog if only he didn't have to be away for such long shifts.

He hadn't been fishing for a sitter. But she leaped at the chance, insisting on taking care of a dog when he worked.

She narrowed her eyes at him. "Of course not. He simply

wants to please me," she said, then winked at the dog and scooped him up in her arms. Henry rubbed his head against her and shot her that puppy dog look. She shooed Travis to the front door. "Be on your way. I need to spend the next twenty-four hours doting on this little boy."

Travis's stepdad Robert closed the screen door behind him, stepping inside the house briefly to say hello. He sighed heavily at the sight of his wife nuzzling the puppy. "That little guy has her wrapped around his paw."

Travis laughed. "Yeah. He's a chick magnet."

Robert tipped his forehead to the lovey-dovey pair. "You should bring him on stage with you at the fireman's auction. You'd surely win."

His mom's eyes sparkled and she nodded. "Oh that's a great idea! Do that, Travis. You can finally break your Susan Lucci streak."

Travis rolled his eyes. He'd lost out on first prize for three years running in the California Bachelor Fireman's Auction, a fundraising event for volunteer fire departments around the state. "Thanks again for reminding me."

"Don't worry. I'll tutor you on winning. Bookstore owners have all the right moves with the ladies," Robert said, flexing his biceps and preening as he posed to the left with an arm pump, then to the right, to show off his guns.

Travis laughed. Robert wasn't a beefy guy at all. Nor was he handy around the house, hence Travis's regular appearances to fix anything that broke. Robert was, however, an extremely good guy, and he also didn't risk his life every day, which helped his appeal in the eyes of his mother after losing Travis' firefighter dad to a blaze long ago.

"Thanks again for watching Henry, Mom. I need to take

off for the firehouse."

"Be safe. Hope you have a quiet shift," his mother said, clasping her hand on her heart. She worried about him every day.

"I will, Mom. I'm always safe."

He dropped a kiss on her forehead and said good-bye, stopping briefly to linger in the hallway, where the wall was lined with family photos. An old wedding picture of his parents from years ago, his dad in his dress uniform and his mom in white. A shot of his dad pushing him on a swing. An image of Travis standing next to his father at the river, the two of them fishing. Then there were the blank years — no photos captured for some time, until he was older, finishing high school. Travis missed his dad, but he also missed that time with his mom. It was as if she'd been underwater then, and those years that followed his father's death were the markers in his life. They were the proof, day after day, year after year, of how love could truly break a heart.

His family was hollow, his youth a black hole until he finished high school and his mom emerged from the sadness. He tracked the photos of his senior year. A few football shots as he played wide receiver, a picture of him dealing cards with some of the guys at the firehouse who'd looked out for him. At the end of the wall, a photo of him and Cara snagged his attention — the proverbial prom shot — him in a tux, her in a light blue dress with slim straps, his arm wrapped around her waist, both of them smiling for the camera.

A memory slipped past him: a reel of the two of them dancing under silver disco balls that spun from the ballroom ceiling at the local hotel where prom was held. She'd always loved dancing; she was a free spirit when music played, and she moved as if the notes truly inhabited her. She'd sung along to the faster numbers, then pulled him in close for the slower ones.

Later that night, they'd taken off, leaving the rest of the decked out seniors in a swirl of dust. But not for a hotel room, or one of their homes. They camped out at the end of Miner's Road by the river, in a tent, with a radio playing some of their favorite music as he spent the night with her under the stars. He peered at the photo, as if the image had tugged his emotions back in time, too. He'd been crazy about her when they were younger, his heart beating fast just from being near her.

He scoffed at the memory, shoving it away. He was happy with her then, but that was because they were teenagers. They had a natural expiration date because of their age and their plans. They were heading off to college at opposite ends of the state. They didn't make any silly promises of forever because they both knew it simply wasn't possible.

Not then. Not now.

Being crazy for someone was a recipe for trouble. Besides, a serious relationship didn't suit his lifestyle. He had his work, he had the firehouse, and he had a dog now. He didn't need the problems that some kind of crazy longing for a woman would bring to his life.

He tapped his knuckles on the wall, as if he was saying good-bye to those kinds of feelings, then took off for the firehouse a mile away. He was an hour early for his shift, but that was the plan.

It was time for Smith to pay up. True, Travis hadn't nabbed any additional days of car washing, as he would have if he'd won Smith's "get her to go home with you" challenge.

But he'd landed the lip lock at the club, and since she'd made it damn clear she didn't intend to ever do a thing with him again, he was going to enjoy all he had—his clean ride.

"Be sure to make the hubcap sparkle," he shouted as Smith set to work on the tires.

"Yeah, yeah, yeah. Watch it, or I'll make some bet you can't resist over how badly you'll lose the fireman's auction. Especially since you're one of the few single guys left to enter."

"No way am I losing this year. No fucking way," Travis said. He wasn't simply trying to win for male pride. He had a more important goal in mind this year, and he desperately wanted to meet it.

• • •

Twenty-four hours later, he finished his shift. As was their habit, he and his buddy Jackson stopped at Becker's bar, The Panting Dog, on the way home. Travis couldn't resist the burger special, complete with extra jalapenos and hot sauce.

"Man, I am looking forward to crashing when I get home," Jackson said as he pushed open the door of the bustling bar.

"Same here. Nothing like a good night's sleep after a long shift," he said, because it had been a busy one, with several first responder calls.

As the door swung shut behind them, Travis scanned the crowded eatery, saying hello to a few familiar faces—the woman who ran his favorite coffee shop, McDoodle's, as well as a cop he knew well, Johnny. Then, he spotted a ponytail he'd recognize anywhere. Cara was perched on a stool at the counter, chatting with his sister as they both nibbled on an appetizer of hummus and carrots.

"I'll join you in a second," he said to Jackson, who'd snagged a table that had just been vacated near the window.

He walked over to the women and said hello. "How are you ladies doing tonight?"

"Ladies?" Megan asked, arching an eyebrow. "Sounds like you're talking about Mom. We're no ladies."

She elbowed Cara, and both of them laughed.

He rolled his eyes. "Gals? You prefer gals?"

"We prefer hot, smart, gorgeous women," Cara said, chiming in.

He couldn't agree more, but he wasn't going to compliment the woman he wanted to fuck in the same breath that he complimented his sister, so he moved on. "Anyway, what's going on?" he asked Megan, but his gaze drifted to Cara, and her short skirt, and those bare legs. His mind instantly returned to the club, and he could recall perfectly how she'd felt in his hands, and how sexy she'd sounded as she chased her pleasure. He shifted behind the stool to hide the evidence of his quick arousal.

Down boy.

"That's great," he said when Megan finished, though he had no clue what she'd just told him.

"So I'd better head home. I have a new client coming in tomorrow morning for a heart and arrow tattoo, and I need to finish the sketch work," Megan added. Ah, she'd been talking about work. Megan had recently opened Hidden Oaks' first tattoo parlor, Paint My Body, and she'd been quickly growing her business.

"I need to head out, too," Cara said, reaching into her

purse to grab some cash. "I'll take care of the bill."

Megan laughed and pressed her hand on top of Cara's. "Stop it. You know Becker won't let me pay. You came in with me, so it's on the house."

"I'll leave a generous tip, then," Cara said as she dipped her hand into her purse.

Travis fished some greenbacks from his wallet. He beat Cara to the punch, reaching between the women to lay the money on the counter. "Tip's on me."

"Thank you, Travis," Cara said, and dropped her hand to his arm, squeezing it. She'd done that before. It was *her* gesture, her way of saying she appreciated something, and even that small touch turned him on. Being so near to her was dangerous, especially since she'd laid down the law the other day. But he couldn't seem to resist. She was to him what peanut butter was to his dog. "Oh, and I wanted to tell you, for Henry's lessons, I think he could benefit from a Martingale collar," she added.

"What's that?"

"Do you have a second? I have one in my car. I'll show you."

"Sure," he said, and as Megan excused herself to say goodbye to Becker, Travis told Jackson he'd join him in a minute.

He followed Cara outside to her car. His eyes strayed to the curves of her ass, so damn tantalizing. Next, her bare legs. God bless summer, and the skin women showed in the warmer months. Her legs were toned and strong, perfect for wrapping around his waist as he drove into her.

He inhaled sharply, trying hard to rewire his brain when he was near her.

Hard being the operative word.

She craned her neck to look up at the dark blanket of night. "I love how clear the sky is here. You can see all the stars," she said, pointing as they walked.

Stars. That would definitely take his mind off his hard-on. "Yeah, I think that's the green dipper right there," he said, deadpan, squinting as if he were studying the twinkling lights against the inky backdrop of night.

"Green dipper?" she asked.

He stroked his chin. "Isn't that what it's called? Or is it the jalapeno dipper nowadays?" he offered up, because he had jalapenos on his mind.

She laughed, then quickly played long. "Actually, it's the Nacho Dipper. It was renamed recently."

"And over there," he said, reaching his arm up high, in the direction of three bright stars in a line, "that's Orion's Suspenders."

She pointed at a shining star. "And isn't that Cleopatra right by the Jalapeno Dipper?"

He patted her back, as if he were proud of her. "You are a damn fine astronomer, Cara," he said as they reached her car, and she flashed him a wide smile.

"You are very clever," she said as she unlocked the front door and stretched across the seat to grab something.

There went his focus-on-the-pretty-stars-in-the-sky plan. Like that, back bent, ponytail spilling over her shoulder, she was in a perfect position for him to take her. To hike up that skirt, learn what color panties she had on tonight, and then tear them off.

She turned around and dropped a dog collar into his hand. "There. Something like this will help him learn all his new tricks faster. Take this to the pet store and get one in his size."

With the speed of a racecar driver, she said a quick good-bye and drove off into the night, leaving him with a hard-on and a dog collar.

As he headed back into The Panting Dog, it occurred to him that both man and dog would need to learn some new tricks. But, he realized, new tricks might be the perfect way to win the fireman's auction.

He'd just need some help from Cara.

Chapter Six

The scent of a fruity hairspray drifted past her nose.

Her sister was putting the finishing touches on Alycia Andrews's sleek new bob. Alycia managed the Silver Pine winery and its popular tasting room on the town square.

"I love the new cut," Cara called out as she walked over to her sister's booth in the local hair salon.

Alycia flashed her a bright smile. "What color are you doing today, Cara? Are you going all purple?"

"Yes, I think it's time for me to match the vines," she said.

Her six-month pregnant sister playfully shot her client a dirty look. "Don't be planting those silly ideas in her head," the chestnut-haired Stacy said, wagging her finger at Alycia.

Alycia held up her hands as if to say, *Who me?*

"I take full responsibility for all my silly ideas. Every single one of them," Cara said, tapping her temple.

"By the way, our new pinot noir is to die for. Stop by

later, and I'll give you a bottle," Alycia said, and then eyed Stacy's belly in apology. "And in a few months for you."

Stacy smiled.

"I'll definitely pop in," Cara said, as Stacy unbuttoned the black smock, folded it up, and swiveled Alycia around to show her the back of her hair in a red handheld mirror.

"Perfect," Alycia said, lightly brushing her new length with her fingertips as she stood up, thanked Stacy, and headed to the front of the salon to pay.

Stacy patted the chair. "Your turn. And don't think you can do that snip-and-dash with me like you did last time."

Cara rolled her eyes. "I always *try* to pay you," she said, indignant.

Stacy ruffled her hair. "I'm just teasing you. You know your money's no good here. So what can I do you for today?"

Stacy was an absolute whiz at hair and always had been. That might even have been the main reason she liked the late addition to the family. When Cara appeared in her life, Stacy had twenty-four hour access to hair to style, to brush, and to play with. She practiced all her techniques on Cara over the years, from temporary color to new twists and chignons. Not to mention a range of cuts and styles from multi-layered, to news anchor length, to this-is-so-short-I'll-kill-you, to long, sleek and sexy, as Stacy referred to it now. Her business at the salon had picked up in recent months, about the time another stylist had left town after a scandal with a married man.

Cara met Stacy's eyes in the mirror. "Can you make me a redhead?" she asked, because she'd cycled through the other major colors in the last year and was ready for a new look. She liked change, and mixing it up. Perhaps that's why she and Stacy had achieved this perfect symbiosis—Cara was a willing guinea pig.

Though sometimes Cara wondered if she'd gone along with Stacy's big sister edicts when they were younger because she had wanted to fit in with the Bailey family. Perhaps she'd been determined to show how well she belonged by happily going with the program. Her parents had treated her just the same as her sisters, but Cara had always been aware that she hadn't joined the family the same way. Maybe that had made her more eager to be like the other girls, and to do what they did, whether it was having her hair done by Stacy, or her clothes picked out by Sofie, who'd always been the fashionista of the bunch. A vintage dress designer with a small Etsy shop, Sofie had used Cara to try out patterns when they were kids.

Nowadays, Cara simply loved having her hair done, and she adored picking out pretty dresses all by herself. Whatever had driven her in her younger years had become the core of who she was today. No point psychoanalyzing herself. She was who she was.

"You made me this way. You addicted me to your crazy styles," she added.

"Fair enough. But we can't go from this shade of dark to redheaded that quickly," Stacy said, picking up a few strands of Cara's hair. "You need to strip out the dark color first, and that'll take some time. Can we do red streaks instead?"

Cara shrugged happily. "Works for me."

"So give me the report. How was the date with Joe? And how was the bachelor-bachelorette party?" Stacy asked, as she mixed the color at the sink next to her booth.

Cara sighed, and shared the details of her lust-free date

with Joe, then her lust-fueled hallway tryst a few nights before with Travis, then how much she'd wanted him last night when she gave him the dog collar. Every encounter with him had her hormones skyrocketing.

"Travis is hot as hell, but Joe's a good guy. He even told me what a nice time he'd had, and how he wants to see me in a few weeks when he's back in town," Cara added as she finished the story. "I really think I should give him another chance."

Stacy gave her the side-eyed stare. "Why? Because you think he's the type of guy you 'should' like?"

"Well, yeah," she said. It seemed obvious that she needed to try harder to stir up some desire for Joe, or someone like him. He wanted the same things, and if she could jumpstart her interest in him then she could be on her way to having all the things she longed for. Her sisters' happiness was inspiring, and she craved a life like that, full of love, family, and kids someday—hopefully someday soon. She'd lived her life so far like her sisters and her parents, and she wanted to be able to give a child all the things that her birth mom hadn't been able to do for her.

She didn't fault her birth mom, but she wanted the opposite—a plan, a roadmap, a guide for how to have a family. She wasn't sixteen and still in high school; she was nearly thirty and owned a business. She just needed a man. As a family guy, Joe possessed all the right raw ingredients. "He's a great guy and we want the same things. I'm sure in time those other elements would develop."

"You mean Mr. Furniture is perfect on paper but you don't feel a spark?" Stacy asked as she grabbed some tinfoil sheets for the highlights.

Cara gulped and nodded. She didn't intend to lie to her sister. "Yep. That's pretty much a good way to sum it up."

Stacy began separating strands of Cara's hair and applying the highlights with a paintbrush. "And that's partly because Mr. Fireman gave you the finger-banging of your life a few nights before."

Cara's eyes widened. "Stacy!"

"Oh hush. No one's here but us. Besides, how do you think this happened?" she said, gesturing to the basketball-sized shape she was sporting.

"Not through finger-banging," Cara said, deadpan.

Stacy rolled her eyes and patted Cara's shoulder. "Obviously. And while I completely understand wanting to give Mr. Perfect another shot, and I think that's an admirable goal, I have an idea to keep you occupied in the meantime."

"What's that?" she asked curiously, eager to learn what her sister was cooking up.

"Everything you need to wash that fireman right out of your hair."

As she rinsed out the conditioner, her sister laid out a plan. Cara's lips twitched in a devilish grin, and she didn't know why she hadn't thought of something like that before, but it was borderline brilliant.

• • •

Was it acceptable to drink wine at a dog training session? Hell no.

But Cara had a feeling she'd need a big fat glassful if she was truly going to go through with Stacy's plan. She grabbed her biggest purse: the huge purple vinyl bag with silver stitching. The fun colors kept it from looking like a feedbag for a horse, even though it was approximately that size. She wrapped a hand towel around the pinot noir, then tucked it into the bag amidst a paperback, her wallet, a bottle of nail polish, her makeup case with a travel toothbrush and toothpaste, various dog leashes and collars, along with a bag of treats in the side compartment. Surely, a drink once she was off the clock would be fine, and he'd be game, she suspected.

She stopped in front of the scalloped pewter mirror in the doorway for one final primp. She fluffed out her new red-streaked hair, smacked her lips so her pink lip gloss spread evenly, and ran a hand down the front of the clingy powder-blue V-neck T-shirt that hugged her curves, smoothing it out over her jean shorts. The wardrobe looked suitable for the gig, but still pretty and feminine.

What truly mattered was what was underneath. That's what had captured his attention the other night, and she wanted to give the man what he liked. The demi-cup bra was a dark pink satin, outlined with black lace, and finished with a bow between the cups. The strap of the bra was a tiny bit visible with the way the shirt fell. That's how she wanted it. Just a little peekaboo for him.

"Perfect," she said to her reflection, then patted Violet on the smooth fur of her head and told her to be good. The border collie mix leaned into her palm then wagged her tail. Cara locked the door, hopped in her car, and headed to Travis's house. She always scheduled the initial sessions at a client's home, because that's where dogs needed to first learn to be on their best behavior.

Her heart sped up as she turned onto his block, and her palms were sweating. She wanted to blame the high eighties of this hot June evening, but she knew it wasn't any fault of the great ball of fire in the sky that she was nervous. It was because she was about to propose something completely out of character for Cara Bailey.

Ready or not, here goes nothing.

She breathed in deeply as she cut the engine in his driveway, then cursed under her breath when she saw him waiting on the porch, leaning casually against the railing on the steps, looking cool and relaxed. Damn, she hadn't been ready to see him yet, and she didn't even have a second to collect herself in her car before she went inside. But then, as she stepped out of her green Mini Cooper, she was no longer thinking of what to say, or how to say it, or when to break out the wine. She was thinking she hoped the next hour flew by because she was dying to get her hands underneath that navy blue T-shirt, tug it over his head, and run her hands across his hard chest.

She wanted her turn to play with his body, and she wanted it ASAP. That was the one clear-cut, reasonable, thoughtful strategy to deal with the pesky lingering desire she felt for him.

"I have something for you," he said as she reached him.

The sun shone brighter in the sky. The birds chirped louder. She was such a sucker for that sweet, thoughtful touch in a guy. But then, who wasn't? "You do?"

He nodded, and handed her a white box, the kind from a bakery. "It's no big deal. Just something from the biscuit bandit. He felt bad for stealing."

Cara clutched the box to her chest, as if she treasured it. "He didn't have to do that, but it's very sweet of your dog to give me a replacement."

Travis shrugged a shoulder. "He's a very sweet dog, as you'll see."

"I have no doubt that he takes after his person," she said, lowering her voice even though it was only the two of them outside under the still-strong evening sun.

Travis scowled. "No one ever accused me of being sweet."

She squeezed him gently on the arm. "Maybe I think you are," she said and there was no masking the flirtation in her voice.

"I better work harder, then, at getting you to see me as something other than sweet," he said, pushing a hand through his dark hair. A note of longing played in her chest. Oh, how she wanted that hand to be hers. How she craved the feel of his hair sliding between her fingers.

"If you don't want me to see you as sweet, how do you want me to see you?"

"Ask me at another time and maybe I'll tell you," he said with a sly wink.

She took heart that he was still as flirty as he'd ever been. That emboldened her for her big question.

"For now, tell the biscuit bandit that I say thank you. And tell him too that I completely understand his desire to steal treats, being a big fan of baked goods myself."

Travis arched an eyebrow. "You don't have to give those to the dogs if you don't want. They're from that bakery in Calistoga. You know that fancy dog bakery? They make the biscuits that dogs and owners can share."

She snapped her fingers. "Yes! The one with the slogan 'This is so good you'll want to eat them too?'"

He nodded. "That's the one. I was down there this afternoon for an executive game with some vineyard guys. I have to go back tonight to prep them for their tournament."

She flipped open the top and brandished a bone-shaped biscuit. She bit into it. "Tastes like peanut butter," she said with a smile, offering him a bite.

"Better than, say, tasting like chicken." He tried the biscuit, and then ran a hand across his belly, making a sound of utter delight as he polished it off. "Don't tell Henry we're keeping them all for ourselves," he whispered, and her heart threatened to cartwheel at the way he said *we*, as if there were a *we* to them.

"Speaking of, we should get started," she said, returning to her professional voice.

He gestured to the front door, swiveling around to open it. Then he whipped his head back. His eyes roamed over her, as if he were seeing her for the first time. His brow knit together in curiosity.

"What is it?" she asked, hoping everything was okay.

He stepped closer, lifted his hand, and fingered a strand of her hair.

Her damn belly did a swan dive as he touched her. He was so close she could inhale that earthy smell of his cologne, like rainwater...subtle and intensely sexy.

"Your hair," he said softly, the volume on his voice turned way down, the tone in it intimate. "It's different."

She drew a breath, as if that would center the wobbliness she felt inside. But the added oxygen only intensified the thrumming in her body, spreading through her veins and leaving a deep longing in its path.

"Red," she said, in a voice that sounded like it was coming from a dream. "My sister did red streaks for me."

His fingers threaded through a strand of her hair, drawing

it between his thumb and forefinger. Her knees nearly buck-led, and her hand shot out to the railing to steady herself. God, she loved having her hair touched by him. It was like some secret location on a treasure map. X marked the spot. One touch and she unraveled.

He shook his head in admiration, drawing a deep breath, as if he were breathing her in. "It looks good. Everything looks good on you."

Chapter Seven

Travis had always known that Cara was good with dogs.

Obviously.

But he had only known that because it was her job. He'd never actually seen her work with a pooch, just as she'd never actually seen him put out a fire. But now, an hour later, Henry lay on the floor of his kitchen, his belly stretched across the cool tile, his eyes fluttering closed, as he drifted off into doggy dreamland. He was spent from the lesson.

Perfect timing.

Travis wasn't nervous, but he wanted to make sure that Cara actually had enjoyed working with his dog before he popped his question. Judging from the progress the stubborn little guy had made in only one hour with her—he was now sitting on command most of the time—he bet she'd be game to help. Travis pulled out a chair at the kitchen table and offered her a beer.

"Or we could have a glass of wine?" she asked, her voice

rising.

Travis wasn't a wine drinker. But he knew that when a woman wanted to have a glass of wine with you, it was usually a good sign of her interest. It was even better when she brought the bottle, because she had reached into her purse and produced a pinot noir from Silver Pine.

Wait.

He wasn't supposed to be thinking of her like that, in terms of interest. He had to narrow in on his mission—the fireman's auction and the help he needed from her—not try to read anything into a bottle of wine, like whether it was a prelude to something more.

She'd made it clear there was nothing more.

"Let me get you a glass," he said, reaching into a cupboard. He passed it to her, then tracked down a rarely-used corkscrew in a kitchen drawer. He reached for the bottle. But as she handed it to him, it nearly slipped from her fingers. He grabbed it quickly before it crashed to the floor in a crimson blur. Fast reflexes came in handy.

"Sorry about that. I keep meaning to get these replaced with the drop-proof variety," she said, holding up her hands.

He laughed at her dry sense of humor. "Nah. Keep them. We'll make it a game. You keep trying to drop things and I'll see what I can catch. Reminds me of my football days," he said as he unscrewed the cork.

"You're on." She dipped her hand into her purse, fishing around in that giant bag. She retrieved a bottle of nail polish, dangled it for a flash, then let it fall.

He lunged, grabbing it before it splattered on the floor, and clutched it in his fist. "Damn. That was impressive."

Her eyes lit up as he dropped the nail polish into her

hand. "It was. You move fast."

"No. I meant you. Impressive how you just went for it. I didn't think you were really going to take me up on that."

She arched an eyebrow. "You like challenges, don't you? I couldn't resist."

"I do like challenges. And you do, too. If memory serves, weren't you the one Alycia Andrews challenged to a rousing rendition of 'All I Want for Christmas Is You' at the holiday party at her wine shop a few years ago?"

Cara's eyes widened. Then she dropped her face into her hands in mock embarrassment. When she lifted her forehead, she peered at him through spread fingers. "Now you're teasing me for my singing skills."

He laughed deeply as he poured a glass of wine and handed it to her. "Hardly. I thought you did a damn fine job belting that out in that little Christmas singing competition, and moving your hips, too. You were always a good dancer."

She shook her head as if she couldn't quite believe she'd done it. But he could remember it clearly—her brazen willingness to grab a mic and sing her heart out, complete with the final finger-point-at-the-whole-damn-crowd at the end of the tune. She had a fearless side that he admired. She didn't seem afraid of anything, and that's how she had sung—with everything she had.

He reached inside the fridge, grabbed a bottle of beer, and opened it. "Bet you sing in the shower, too."

She raised an eyebrow and shot him a naughty look. "Wouldn't you like to know?"

"Oh hell yeah. I'd like to know."

"Do you? Sing in the shower?" she asked, turning the tables on him.

He put on a straight face, feigning intense solemnity as he joined her at the table. "No. I take my showers very seriously. I am all business," he said, and when she laughed, he wanted to pump a fist. He wasn't sure why he felt that way, but he sure did like making her laugh. Always had. Maybe because she had a pretty laugh, just like she had a pretty voice.

Then she surprised him by singing a line from what distinctly sounded like a Taylor Swift type tune. "That's what I sang in the shower this morning. It was blasting on the local radio station, so I sang along."

He raised an eyebrow and held up his beer. "Very impressed."

She held up the glass to toast. "To showers. Music. And to well behaved dogs," she said, eyeing Henry.

He clinked his bottle against hers. "I will drink to all of that. And speaking of dogs, and speaking of challenges. I have a special request, Cara."

She took a swallow of the wine. "Okay, what's the request?"

"I'm in the California Bachelor Fireman's Auction in two weeks. I've done it for the last few years, and…" He paused and held up his thumb and forefinger to show a sliver of space. "I'm *this* close to winning first prize."

She furrowed her brow. "You've never won?"

He shook his head, heaving a frustrated sigh. He forced his lips into an exaggerated pout. "It's embarrassing." He hung his head in pretend shame.

She patted his thigh. "There, there," she said playfully.

But her fingers on him didn't make him feel playful at all. They sent his mind reeling with images he was going to have to push far, far away if his plan was going to work. As his eyes strayed to her hand on his leg, he tried to buckle in his own desires. His instincts were blaring like a siren, telling him to clasp her hand, to draw her close, to turn the slightest touch from her into a whole lot more, into her wrapping those luscious legs around him, sinking down on him, and riding him right here, right now, her hair flowing down her spine as she called out his name. Great. Now he was rock hard. What was he thinking, wanting to spend more time with her to prep for the auction? Being in the same vicinity with the woman he wanted but couldn't have was like sending someone on a diet to infiltrate the Ben & Jerry's factory.

But hell, he wanted to win, and he had his reasons. He focused on the task at hand, doing his best to ignore the tempting memories of the other night and the repeat he wanted of it right now.

"Here's the deal with the fireman's auction. In addition to whatever the winning bid is for the top man, first place also gets five thousand dollars, and the prize goes to a fire-related charity of the winner's choosing. And I want to win big to give it to the Families of Fallen Firefighters," he said, speaking crisply so he wouldn't choke up on why it meant so much to him.

She straightened her spine and nodded. "Of course. That's a great charity."

"Yeah. It is. Their support helped my mom. Their survivors' network made a big difference for her when she was struggling, even a few years after my dad died. Some of the others who'd been through the same kind of loss helped pull her out of the depression she battled for a while there. The problem is, they've been hurting for a few years for funds, and this year has been particularly tough for the charity.

They've had to cut back on the one-to-one support services for families, and on the counseling. But they've found a few small businesses that have put up some money, and an insurance broker has even offered to match any donations of five thousand or more. So with the prize and the match, that could make a big difference."

He'd given money before to the cause, and while he had a nice savings account, he didn't have the kind of stability in his job to peel off those funds all by himself. This auction was his big chance. "So I want to win the big prize and give back even more to them." The moment bordered on solemn, as Cara fixed him with a serious stare and blinked back the start of a tear. He cleared his throat. "And I'm hoping you can help."

"Absolutely," she said, scooting her chair closer. His heart dared to skip a beat with the certainty of her answer. He hadn't even shared details, and she'd already said yes. "What do you need?"

A small laugh escaped his throat. He was about to turn a serious moment into a light-hearted one, but he hoped he was talking Cara's language. He knocked back a swallow of his beer, and then set the bottle down amidst a mess of papers and magazines on his table. "Here's the thing. I'm pretty sure Henry can help me win first prize."

She knit her eyebrows together. "How?"

He tipped his forehead to the sleeping puppy, curled up like a comma by the kitchen doorway. "That right there is a top-notch chick magnet," he said, and Cara cracked up instantly, peals of laughter rippling through the evening air that drifted in from the open porch door.

"He is absolutely a chick magnet," she agreed. "I bet

when you take him for a walk in the town square, all the ladies are stopping to talk to you."

He nodded. There was just something about a puppy that reeled in women of every age, and that canine knew how to work them with his big-brown-eyed charm and wagging tail. "My plan is this. I want to bring him on stage with me for the auction. He's my secret weapon. We'll be the dog and the fireman, and I'm pretty sure I can nab the top prize and give the Families of Fallen Firefighters the funds they need to keep up their work."

"You'd be irresistible with him," she said, in that soft, flirty tone she'd used at the club. The sound of it set his blood racing and made him shift in the chair because matters below the belt were becoming infinitely harder.

He nearly smacked his own forehead to knock some sense into it. He was walking straight into temptation. Hell, he was knocking on the damn door and begging to be tortured by this woman. She was so damn sexy and funny, and so off-limits by her own admission.

But here he was, sticking his foot in that door, asking for more. "Irresistible?"

"Very much so," she said, then grabbed her glass. She drained the rest of her wine. He ignored his beer. He needed to drive down to Calistoga in about—he glanced at the stark black and white clock on the wall—twenty minutes.

"So I take it you need my services to make sure that your guy is ready to go on stage. That he's perfectly behaved, and will look absolutely adorable next to you, so the women can't resist bidding on a date with the hottest single fireman in all of California," she said, and he squeezed his eyes shut briefly at hearing those words.

Sure, he craved challenges, but this was testing him something fierce, as she dropped compliments left and right, which made his fingers itch to grab her, pin her down, and have her again and again. And he was the idiot walking straight into it, knowing he was going to spend even more time with the one woman who'd made it patently clear she was hands-off from here on out.

Even so, he fanned the flames of the fire. "Hottest in all of California?"

She nodded, and poured more wine for herself. "You know I think that, Travis. And I'm more than happy to help you and Henry win it all."

"The auction is in two weeks, so we'd need to do lessons more than once a week. I'm thinking we should get together every other day," he said, reaching for a canister of gasoline and watching the flames lick the sky now.

"That sounds great," she said as she crossed her legs, kicking a foot back and forth, all cool and casual. His eyes were drawn to her feet; he wasn't a foot man, but every single thing about this woman was pretty, down to the blue polish on those toenails. "I'm in," she said with a bright smile.

This was almost too easy. He'd been expecting some friction, some kind of pushback, given the lines in the sand she'd drawn at the park. He didn't expect her to so easily say yes. But maybe she'd snuffed out her desire for him. Fine, if she could rein in the urge, he could damn well do the same. Play it cool. Keep it all on the level.

"In fact," she added, as she ran her finger along the rim of her wineglass, "it works perfectly with the favor I wanted to ask you."

He held out his arms wide. "Anything. You're helping

me. I'll do anything I can."

"Great," she said, and took one more sip of wine. A hearty sip. A big fat fucking gulp. Hell, was she going for liquid courage? Because she'd plowed through nearly two glasses in the span of fifteen minutes, and it sure seemed like she was fonder of wine tonight than he'd remembered. "Because here's what I want."

She scooted her chair closer, ran a hand through her hair, then met his eyes. Her voice was both sultry and drop-dead clear as the next words fell from her glossy lips. "I want to finish what we started at the club. I want you to fuck me six ways to Sunday. I want to stop daydreaming about more sex with you and start having it."

If he'd been doing the dishes, a plate would have slipped from his hand, shattered into shards. If he were strolling along the sidewalk, he'd have stumbled in surprise. Instead, he scrubbed his hand over his jaw, narrowed his eyes, and said, "Come again?"

He had to be hearing things.

Her blue eyes sparkled, a naughty look in them as her lips curved upward. "Yes. That. Coming again and again."

He'd walked right into a pun. *"Now?"* he asked, still in shock from the way she'd echoed her words from the dog park, the thing she swore they couldn't do. This had to be a joke. Maybe a bet. Maybe she was giving him a taste of his own medicine from the other night.

"Sure. That'd be a good start. And maybe the next day and the next and the next. But not forever. Just for, say, a few weeks? Up until the auction would probably be sufficient. We could even line up this fling with the dog training."

He peered around the corner, leaning back in his chair,

as if he were scanning for a candid camera 'gotcha' moment. "Is Megan here? Is Jamie? Is this some kind of payback?"

She shook her head. "No. Why? You don't want to have a fling with me?"

He nodded vigorously. "Oh, I want it. I want that more than you can even know. But are you for real? Is this a joke? Or a prank?"

She narrowed her eyes. "I ask you to sleep with me, and you think I'm pranking you? Give me more credit than that," she said with a huff.

He reached for her hands, laced his fingers through hers. "I will give you all the credit in the world. Just tell me, is this a real question?"

She nodded, and there was no teasing in her eyes, no playing around, just a sweet, vulnerable, and honest look. "I want you," she whispered, "so much it drives me crazy. But I know you don't do relationships. This is no commitment, no dating, no fuss, no muss. Two weeks while we train Henry, and then we're done." She wiped one palm against the other to show it would be a clean break at the end.

"So you want dog training and sex?" he asked, still sure he was hearing things—like, his wildest fantasies coming true.

"Yes. The perfect combo."

"Okay. And not that I'm protesting, because let me make it clear, my answer is yes, fuck yes, and absofuckinglutely yes, but why the change?"

She let go of his hands to stand up, then sank back down, straddling him. Oh, hell. There went any breathing room in his jeans. His dick did its best approximation of a flagpole.

She cupped his shoulders, looking him square in the eyes. Being this close to her was dizzying, and an absolute rush. "Because, Travis, I can't get you out of my head. Or my body. I went on a date the other night with the nicest guy around. I think there could be something real with him," she said, and he bristled and nearly breathed fire. The image of her on a date with someone else made his gut twist. "But all I could think about when I was out with him was sleeping with you and all the ways I want to have sex with you." His head was fever hot. A tremor of lust slammed into him, and he grasped her waist, digging his fingers into her hipbones.

"There are so many ways I want to have you, Cara," he whispered, hot and rough against the delicate skin of her throat, savoring the way gooseflesh rose instantly on her skin.

"And that's what I need. You gave me the best sex of my life, starting way back when we were in high school, which is crazy in and of itself. But so it goes, and no one compares to you. Not that I have a ton of experience, but the way I see it is, I will never be able to move on and have the dream—the white picket fence, and the family, and all those things I want—if I'm still thinking of how good it is with you."

"Don't forget about the time after college graduation on the picnic table in the woods by the river. And then that night three years ago when you were back in town for Alycia's holiday party, and I kissed you under the mistletoe at the party after you sang that song, and you pulled me into a coat closet and insisted on having me right then and there," he said.

She dropped her face into her hands. "See? That's my point," she muttered, and then looked up at him. "All those times are messing with my head. And I can't seem to connect with anyone else because I'm hung up on you. So the only conclusion I can come to is, if I'm ever going to meet Mr.

Right, I need to get Mr. Wrong out of my system."

Sweeter words were never uttered by a woman. Because this was a dream come true. Cara was his fantasy girl, but she was more than a fantasy. He'd had her, and he knew just how good it was when the two of them were together. He slipped his fingers under her shirt. She trembled at his touch and his hands traveled north, seeking out those wondrous breasts, which damn near seemed to be calling his name. "So you need to fuck me to stop wanting to fuck me?"

She leaned her head back in a yes, her throat long and inviting. So feminine, so enticing, and so primed for hot kisses. He blazed a trail up the column of her throat as she answered him with the hottest words ever: "Fuck me hard, and fuck me slow, and fuck me wild."

That sounded more like a recipe for wanting more sex, but Travis wasn't going to protest. He was dying to slide into her wet heat, to feel her body take him deep and shudder beneath him. "And that's all you want?"

"That's all I want. Well, I do like it when you get all bossy and tell me what to do, so I want that too," she said, pulling back to shoot him a mischievous look as she trailed her fingertips down his chest. His breath hitched. "I want your body, and I want to walk away when we're done."

He yanked her closer, her chest slamming against his as he nibbled on her earlobe, drawing out a moan. Then he bit down. She yelped lightly, and he soothed out the sting with his tongue. "You can have anything you want with me. You name it. You tell me how you want to get me out of your system, and I will deliver it," he said, and flicked open the button on her jean shorts. She gasped as he tugged down the zipper. "But first, you're going to strip for me. So stand up and take these off."

She scooted away from him, kicking off her sandals then dipping her thumbs into the waistband of her shorts.

"Take them off slowly as you look at me. Don't rush a damn thing. I want to know that you're undressing just for me. Show me how much you want this," he instructed, leaning forward, parking his elbows on his thighs as he savored the gorgeous sight before him. Cara, stripping in his kitchen, giving him that wild look that undid him. Like she'd done at the club. Like she did at the Panting Dog all the times he bumped into her there. Like she'd done every moment they'd been together. When they were alone, she ditched the fun, sweet, quirky hometown girl she also was, and turned into this naughty woman who craved dirty sex with him.

"You sure you want them off all the way?" she asked, tilting her head and batting those eyelashes.

"Positive."

"Like this?" She inched one side down over her hip, a sliver of her panties peeking out. Dark pink. Sinfully hot.

"More. All the way off."

"If you say so."

"I do say so. Show me what you wore for me."

She stopped undressing and gave him a chiding look. "How do you know I wore something just for you?"

"Because you came here to seduce me. You came here with a plan. You were armed with a proposition you knew I couldn't resist. And I bet you chose your weapons wisely," he said, arching an eyebrow as he reached his fingers to the patch of pink lace that she'd revealed. He hooked his thumb underneath and brushed the pad against her hipbone, watching as she drew a sharp breath. "All the way off, now. Let me see."

"Tell me if my weapons work at disarming you, Travis. Tell me if they make you want to take me right now and throw me down on your bed," she said as she pushed her shorts over her hips, down to her thighs…and oh holy fucking hotness.

His dick pounded against his jeans, and he stopped moving. Just stared at her panties. They were pink, black, lacy, and so damn enticing. His throat was parched. He lowered his head, bending to her waist so he could brush his lips against the fabric. A delicious moan fell from her mouth to his ears. He ran his finger between her legs. She was so wet that the pads of his fingers were damp. A landslide of want tumbled through his body.

"Cara, you're going to need to wear sexy lingerie every day for the next few weeks, because it drives me absolutely wild. Everything you do does."

She bit her lip, then said in a sexy, husky voice, "That's exactly why I wore them."

He tugged her shorts off the rest of the way, and she stepped out of them.

"But let me make one thing clear," he said.

"Yes?"

"I'm not taking you on the bed. You didn't come to me with this proposition so I could hold your hand like a blushing schoolboy and walk you back to my bedroom, then dim the lights, put on soft music, and do it all slow and gentle."

"You're right. I didn't come to you for that."

"You came to me because you know we've never bothered to wait for beds," he said, running his hands down her bare legs. "And if you want to get me out of your system, it's going to happen everyplace but the bedroom. Get on my table. We'll start there."

He shoved the magazines and papers in one swift move, letting them tumble to the floor. Henry lifted his head in curiosity, then rose and trotted out of the kitchen as if he were giving them their privacy. Perfect. Travis picked up Cara and set her on the edge of the table. Then he slid his hands under her ass and inched off those panties, his breath catching in his chest and all the blood in his body diverted to his dick once more as he watched her laid bare before him. Her beautiful bare pussy glistened with desire, ready for him.

Chapter Eight

Propped on her elbows, half-naked, perched on his kitchen table, she was a live wire.

So ready.

His eyes raked over her. Her shirt and bra were still on, but he didn't seem to care because he was fixated between her legs now, staring at her, his eyes hooded with lust. He pressed his palms on the edge of the table and dipped his head closer, closer, closer. Oh God. She dropped her head back on her shoulders as his breath ghosted over her. His mouth was so deliriously near to where she ached madly for him.

She shuddered before he even touched her. She'd fly to the moon any second. One touch and she'd launch into orbit.

His tongue flicked softly on the inside of a thigh, and she cried out. He groaned appreciatively. "Love those sounds you make. I don't want you to ever be quiet with me," he said as he kissed her, making his way to the V of her legs.

"That shouldn't be a problem," she said, then moaned again as he traveled up her flesh.

He took his time, his stubbled jaw brushing against her skin, his face inching near, until he was so close she was sure that was the moment he'd put her out of her misery and kiss her. Just kiss, and lick, and eat, and fucking claim her with his mouth.

Please.

But instead, he darted to her other leg, bestowing the same lingering, soft kisses there. Killing her with desire. Red-hot, ratcheting-up-the-scale-to-the-sky want. Then, he pressed his hands against her inner thighs and parted her legs wide. "This is how I want you," he whispered.

"Please. You can have me any way you want." She arched her hips, willing him to kiss her, begging with her body for him to touch her.

He licked.

Once.

That was all. One long, slow, agonizingly intense stroke up her wet center, then a hard flick against her throbbing bundle of nerves.

And her body shook with that first stroke.

It was like a promise and a countdown all at once. This was not going to take long. Oh hell no. This was going to be a rocket ride into white-hot bliss.

She gasped and moaned as he licked again, another hot, sweet line that lit her up like a neon sign against the night sky. Then that swirl against her clit that made her cry out again, his name like a song's chorus on her lips. He drew her into his mouth, sucking hard then flicking his tongue up and down, up and down.

She bowed her back, her palms jammed against the wood of the table, her knees up, her body open to him. He stopped for a second to clasp his hands on her ankles. "Let me see more of you," he whispered, briefly breaking contact with the center of her world as he spread her all the way, making her even more vulnerable to him.

He groaned. "Such a beautiful sight. You here for me, wanting to get me out of your system by letting me eat your beautiful pussy," he said, and heat pooled between her legs with his filthy words.

"Travis," she moaned. Every atom in her buzzed as she waited, poised on the edge of a cliff for him to return. He dropped his mouth to the inside of her knee, but she couldn't take any more teasing.

"Does that sweet, sexy way you say my name mean you're about ready to come on my tongue?" he asked, giving her the dirtiest of dirty looks.

"Yes. God yes," she said, then took matters into her own hands as she grabbed his head. Her fingers curled tightly into his hair, her nails cutting into his scalp as she drew him back to her.

His mouth was sinful, his tongue some kind of wondrous, wicked thing as he kissed and licked and sucked. She rocked into him, keeping pace with each tantalizing stroke, each insanely delicious kiss. He scooped his hands under her ass, bringing her closer, and she thrust against him as her vision blurred and her cells blazed. The tension inside her tightened, coiling higher, twisting as she neared that edge, and then he kissed her with his whole mouth, consuming her. She snapped and screamed his name, a tornado of pleasure whipping through her, chasing down all the far corners of her body.

She lived there briefly, residing in that land of pure pleasure, in the druggy delicious afterglow of an orgasm that still rippled through her.

Soon she blinked, coming up for air, as the world shone silvery and bright. She smiled, a woozy, dopey smile, as he rose, grabbing the bottom of his shirt and tugging it over his head. Her breath caught as she gazed at his chest. She'd seen him naked before. Hell, she'd copped a peek at him shirtless just last summer, when she'd been lucky enough to drive by the twisty county road where his sister had shot his photo for the local fireman's calendar. His body was living art, all carved and strong, each muscle outlined like he'd been drawn in a master class.

"Still think I'm sweet?" he asked.

She shook her head. "Nope."

"How do you see me now?"

"Dirty. And I like it that way," she said. She reached for the belt loops on his jeans, trying to sit up even though her head was light, and full of a constellation of scattered, dancing stars.

He shook his head. "Can't right now."

"What?" Shock reverberated in her body. She was ready to stomp her foot and demand he suit up and slide inside her this very second. Who cared that she already came so damn powerfully her body was still vibrating? She wanted more. She wanted him.

"I have to go back to Calistoga to meet some clients who are prepping for a tournament, to watch them play and figure out what they need to do better in their game."

She tipped her chin at his bare chest. "Why'd you take

your shirt off, then?" As if she could catch him in a loophole. Keep him. Take him. *Ride him.*

"I need to change. Put on a button-down. Class it up."

"You are such a tease," she said, frustration thick in her voice. Even though she was the one who was leaving sated, she couldn't help but want more. "And I want to make you come. I feel terribly selfish leaving you like this."

He laughed. "Don't worry about me, you sweet, dirty girl." He bent down, dropped a kiss on her forehead, then her eyelids, then her lips. She could taste herself on him.

"You taste like me," she whispered.

"Then I must taste delicious," he said with a wink. "Oh, and by the way, I fully expect you to get yourself off again tonight after you finish watching Bobby Flay. But don't think of him. Think of me."

Her jaw nearly dropped. "One, I'm not into Bobby Flay. And two, why would you say that?"

He lifted her off the table and handed her the panties. "Because you love your cooking shows. They're like your happy zone, and always have been. You watch them before you get in bed."

Her lips rose in a faint smile. He was spot on, even though she didn't entirely want to admit he knew so many of her little quirks and habits, including her bedtime rituals. "Fine. I *might* watch Food Network. But how can you be so certain I'll be masturbating?"

He brushed his fingers down her bare arm. "Because you want it again. Because you want me to fuck you right now, and I'm not going to. Therefore, my powers of deduction tell me that you'll go home, maybe have another glass of wine, watch a cooking show 'til you're tired, then put on some sexy, lacy camisole thing, get into bed, and still be wet for me. You'll figure you'll sleep better if you take the edge off. So you'll spread your legs. Ride your hand. Call out my name. Then, when I see you in a day, you're going to tell me what you pictured as you were getting off. And I'm going to do that to you."

Her skin sizzled as she dressed. This man could have his way with her. He had her number. He rattled her. He sent her soaring. He made her wild.

"You'll do it? No matter what I fantasize about? Anything?"

He nodded as she pulled on her shorts. "Anything that gets you off will turn me on," he said. "Guaranteed."

Five minutes later, he walked her out. "Give me your keys," he said, holding open his palm.

She furrowed her brow. "Why? Are you coming over later?" Hope sprang in her chest.

"I'm going to be pretty late, so no. But I'm giving you a ride home now, since I want you to get there safely. I've seen too many times the damage that even two glasses of wine can do."

Her heart beat faster from his offer. She teetered just on the edge of tipsy. She hadn't drunk much, but it was better to be safe.

"Thank you."

"And when I get home, I'll drive your car to your house so you'll have it in the morning."

"How will you get home, then?"

"Don't you worry about me," he said, then opened the door to his truck and whisked her off to her house…

Where later that evening she did just as he'd asked.

Chapter Nine

The fire truck gleamed under the noontime sun, polished so brightly it could double as a red mirror.

Travis stepped away to appraise his work, an important part of the daily agenda. Yup, part of the job as a volunteer firefighter in the Hidden Oaks fire department was making sure the engines always represented.

Later today, a group of grade schoolers from a summer camp that conducted daily field trips around the county would be stopping by for a tour of the firehouse. Travis had done his part to make sure the trucks were indeed fire engine red, pristine and crisp as the buttons on a dress uniform. Even the hubcaps shined and the tires were freshly scrubbed. You never knew if today would be the day some young boy or girl would flash back to and say, "That was when I first knew I wanted to be a firefighter."

That was how it had gone for Travis. Sure, his dad had been a card-carrying member of Battalion 654 in this very same town, and that played the largest role in Travis's bone-deep certainty he would follow in his footsteps. But he also could recall with crystal clarity the summer day when he was five and had visited his dad here. Megan was a baby, perched on their mom's hip, and Travis walked next to his mom, holding her hand. She was stopping by one afternoon to bring freshly baked cookies for the men on shift. His dad had wrapped his wife in a hug, dropped a kiss on the baby's forehead, and plunked his fire helmet on his son's head. Then he hoisted Travis up, sat him in his lap on the front seat of the engine, and let him pretend to drive the truck.

Travis had fallen in love at first sight.

He was *that* kid—that one who said, "I want to be a fireman when I grow up," and then did it.

Even losing his dad in the line of duty hadn't quenched his desire. If anything, it had strengthened it. His dad had died saving a family in a fire, and Travis wanted to be able to honor not only his father's sacrifices but also his own sense of duty, community, and giving back. There had never been any question, never any doubt. Even in spite of the things he'd seen on the clock, he'd never once let the shadow of the job fall over him.

Like last night.

He and Jackson were the first responders on scene at a car crash. A few minutes after midnight, they'd pulled a young couple out of a crushed vehicle. The car had skidded off the road, toppled by another vehicle in a hit and run. Whoever smashed into them had vanished into the night, likely weaving down the road from too much wine. That was the reality in Wine Country where they lived and worked— what they lacked in fires they made up for in drunk driving accidents. The man and woman had been bloodied and bruised, knocked unconscious.

That incident was one of the regular reminders that work there in quiet Hidden Oaks wasn't all pancake breakfasts and shiny trucks. But thankfully his buddy in dispatch had called an hour ago to update him that, while broken bones abounded, the injuries were manageable.

That had been a relief.

But whether he was prepping trucks for grade school field trips, or helping at the scene of an accident, Travis was grateful to give back. He tucked away the cloths and cleaning supplies and got ready to head to his mom's house to pick up Henry. On his way out, he spotted Megan and the fire chief, Becker, walking up the street, holding hands. Becker had the next shift. In his free hand, he held a large grocery bag.

"Don't even tell me you made him a lunch and packed it up," Travis said, shaking his head in mock disgust at the happy couple.

Megan parked a hand on her hip and shot him a stare. "Maybe it's not lunch. Maybe I made Mud Pie Brownies for everyone at the firehouse. Except you."

Travis clutched his chest as if she had wounded him. He and Megan had long ago learned to fend for themselves in the kitchen, taking care of meals and cooking. They'd mastered mac and cheese, spaghetti and meatballs, and sandwiches like nobody's business, but their specialties were brownies and cookies. "You're killing me. And you better give me one. You know I can't resist your baking."

"You're the one who taught me how to bake," she said with a laugh, as she ran her hand through her hair, her diamond engagement ring shining in the sun.

"And don't you forget it," he said pulling her in for a quick hug. She dipped her hand into the bag Becker held and produced a brownie. Travis bit into it, and patted his belly in appreciation.

Then Becker clapped Travis on the back. "What's the latest? Anything I need to know about?"

Travis gave his good friend a quick update, including the details on the pending arrival of a few dozen grade schoolers. "So don't be your usual gruff and moody self," Travis teased, even though that side of Becker hadn't made too many appearances since he'd fallen fast and hard for Megan.

"Thanks. I'll do my best impression of Smith," he said, since Smith was the consummate happy-go-lucky guy, making him the perfect ambassador for the fire service. "Speaking of, did you get someone to fill in for you for his wedding?"

Travis had been scheduled for duty that day, along with a few other guys, so they'd called on some of their buddies in a nearby town to fill in so they could all attend the event. "The Whiskey Springs guys will be here to help. Do I need to take care of your wedding plans soon, too? I'm gonna be scheduling tuxes and bachelor parties left and right, with the way my men are falling."

Becker had sworn off love, closeness, and companionship for a lot of the same reasons as Travis had. He'd lost his chief and best friend in a Chicago fire two years ago, and had to leave that city and start over here to escape the memories. Travis had been surprised as hell when the man had gone and fallen hard for his sister, because Becker didn't get close to anyone.

Everything changed when he met Megan.

"With the way you're all toppling like dominoes, you're

making it easier for me to clean up at the California Fire-man's Auction. Two more weeks 'til glory," Travis added.

Becker rolled his eyes. "Let the record reflect that I never competed in that beauty pageant."

"And if he had, he would have won all the prizes." Megan said, clasping an arm around Becker and flashing him a private smile.

"Damn lovebirds," Travis muttered and waved good-bye, then headed to his truck.

Good thing he had a will of iron, unlike those other guys. He could resist falling for a woman. He could resist it so easily.

Right?

He nodded at himself in the rearview mirror as he pulled onto the street.

"Right," he answered, as he found himself counting down the hours until he would see Cara again.

• • •

"May we have the rings?"

Jamie swiveled around, her eyes sparkling under the late afternoon sun that rained heat over the vines, and called out to her dog while Cara watched.

Dutifully sitting twenty feet away, Chance rose and trot-ted to Jamie. "Sit," she instructed and the big dog did as asked, parking himself next to his mistress amidst a row of Merlot grapes, dark blue and primed for a summer crush.

"Then Smith will take the rings from his collar," Cara said, running the bride and groom through the one moment from their ceremony that required her particular brand of expertise. Smith bent down to the dog, reached into a leather pouch attached to the collar, and mimed removing the rings.

"Then, you'll ask Chance to lie down," Cara said, and Jamie gave the big German Shepherd the command. He dropped to his belly, panting and patiently waiting. Cara had known Jamie growing up in this town, but since Cara was a few years older, they didn't become close friends until she started working with Jamie's dog last year. Now, Jamie was one of her favorite people. In a bizarre twist of fate, Cara had actually gone on a couple dates with Smith a few years back, but had ended things quickly because she could tell he had it bad for Jamie.

"And he'll be perfect while we exchange the vows," Smith proclaimed, gesturing to the dog he'd procured from a San Jose shelter a little over a year ago. Chance was a puppy then, and now he was full-grown. As Cara liked to say, Chance was officially "kangaroo sized" since German Shepherds had that loping look to them. She'd helped Smith track down the dog as a gift to Jamie when he was wooing her, had helped him learn all his basic commands, too, and now he was going to be their ring bearer.

"And then when the ceremony is over I'll take him home for you, so you won't have to worry about him at the wedding."

"Perfect," Jamie said.

Pride welled up inside Cara as she flashed back on how far the dog had come in one year, from his early days as a troublemaking pup to his role now as a gentle giant. Some days, she felt like the luckiest person in the world to be able to do what she loved for a living. She'd always felt a kinship with animals, that deep, unconditional love that comes from companionship with four-legged friends. She'd grown up with dogs, and from an early age, she knew she wanted to work with them for a livelihood. But there was more to her business than just her affection for animals. Helping a person and a dog learn how to communicate and meet each other's needs without the benefit of language was truly her joy.

So she was a bit like a proud parent as she beamed at the brown and tan beast at her feet. Besides, it was better to cast her gaze at him than at Smith and Jamie, since the two of them were practicing the "you may now kiss the bride" part of their wedding in two weeks, here in the vineyard that Jamie's parents owned—Ode Wines.

They were a PDA kind of couple, and were always touching and kissing in public. A random thought swooped down—if she and Travis were a couple, would they be like this in public, hands slinking under shirts, lips brushing across bare shoulders? She quickly admonished herself for even letting such a notion visit her conscious mind. She and Travis would never, ever be a couple. She was clearly inhaling secondhand romance fumes from the too-in-love vibes wafting off her friends.

Smith and Jamie were the first among her circle of friends in Hidden Oaks to wed, and they wouldn't be the last. Travis's tattoo artist sister Megan had just started planning with her mom her wedding to Becker. Cara suspected Mrs. Jansen would be quite busy indeed with that event, especially since it was the *only* time she'd likely see one of her children walk down the aisle. Travis was as perennially single as they came, and determined to stay that way. Her heart darkened, as if a cloud had stolen across the sky. She wished he wasn't so dead set against relationships, or so sure they would only inflict pain. Not for her sake, of course. They'd never fit long term. But for *his*. From his dry sense of humor, to his caring heart, to his drop-dead looks, he was quite the catch. She was reminded as much when she'd walked outside yesterday morning to find her car safe and sound in her driveway, her keys tucked in the mailbox, and a note that said, *Hope you slept well.*

She sighed as she walked away from the happy couple, who looked liked they wanted to climb each other.

A minute later, Jamie caught up as Cara wandered into the main tasting room of the vineyard. The room was closed for an hour but would open up again for an evening tasting. "Sorry," Jamie said, blushing as she smoothed a hand over her rumpled tank top.

"Hey, don't apologize. You're supposed to want to kiss the groom, so it's all good," Cara said, flashing a smile. "Where's Chance?"

"Smith is taking him home. I'm famished. Want some olives?"

"Nothing says satisfy-a-hungry-appetite like olives," Cara teased.

Jamie strolled behind the counter in the tasting room, plucking a bowl of olives from the fridge, along with crackers and cheese then setting them on a wooden cutting board for serving.

"So this is the year of the wedding, it seems," Cara said as she hopped onto a stool. "First you and Smith, then Megan and Becker."

"Maybe you're next," Jamie mused, as she pushed a plate of olives to her.

Cara scoffed as she bit into a salty one. "Doubtful. I'd

have to have that thing known as a fiancé first, which would mean I'd need a beau first, which would mean I'd have to go on a decent date first."

She thought of Joe — Mr. Perfect-on-paper. Their date *was* decent. She needed to keep reminding herself of that. She was already surrounded by reminders that she was the last of her friends, and last of her sisters, who was still shooting at the happily ever after.

Jamie shrugged happily as she sliced a cheese knife through some Brie, and popped a piece into her mouth. "Speaking of, how are things going with Travis?" she asked in the most off-hand voice, not even meeting her eyes.

Cara stared at Jamie until her friend peeked up at her from beneath a curtain of blond hair. Jamie had an up-to-something look in her eyes. "You mean, how's the dog training with Henry going?"

"That and anything else," she said evasively.

Had Travis spilled to Smith about their arrangement already? They'd never said the other night that it was top-secret, but still. The connection they shared in the bedroom — well, everywhere *but* the bedroom — was private and personal.

"Has Smith said something to you?"

Jamie's eyes widened. "Is there something to say?"

"No," Cara said, both denying the truth and protecting her privacy at once.

Jamie snapped her fingers. "Darn."

"Why?"

"Because I was really hoping that night at the club would be the start of something for the two of you."

In a way, Cara was too.

"Because…I have a confession," Jamie continued, taking a loud gulp as she lowered her voice. "Smith and I kind of planned it together."

"What?"

"Since both you and Travis are into each other, but wouldn't do a thing about it, we plotted in advance for Smith to make a bet because we knew it would goad Travis," Jamie said, fixing on the kind of smile that said, *Don't be mad at me.*

"You little devil," Cara said, whistling in admiration. "The whole time you acted so surprised, but you'd been playing little miss secret matchmaker."

Jamie nodded, her eyes a confession, her voice now wistful. "I thought it would lead to more."

It *had* led to more. It had led to being eaten like an ice-cream sundae on Travis's kitchen table. But it was best she not say that, since he *did* have friends over for barbecues and whatnot. Probably better that they not know Cara had been an appetizer one evening. She smirked to herself at the memory.

"You went off in la-la land. Got a little secret?" Jamie asked.

Cara blushed. "Just thinking of my to-do list." And Travis's, and how they were both on each other's to-do lists for a few weeks. "I need to go. I'm meeting Travis for a dog training lesson."

"Don't do anything I wouldn't do," Jamie said with a wink, as she popped an olive between her lips.

Cara arched an eyebrow. "That doesn't limit me much, does it?"

"Exactly. And like I was saying, you two just always

seemed to get along so well—you laugh at the same jokes, like the same music, and you're both so outgoing. I just thought you two would be good together. "

"I know," Cara said softly, the words slipping out before she realized they'd made landfall. She froze, then quickly backpedaled, even though Jamie's points were precisely why she and Travis had fallen for each other the first time around. Funny how they'd had an expiration date then, too, since their college plans separated them by distance. Maybe that's why the summer they'd spent together had been so fun, and so romantic in its own way. They both knew they were simply going to make the most of their time together, and that they couldn't have anything more. Clearly, that's all she and Travis were ever destined for. Little slivers of time.

"I mean, he's great, and fun, and we get along well. But I can't ever see us together, since we want such different things, and I respect his choices."

She especially respected the choice he was making to live out her fantasies. Besides, it was so much safer to focus on the sex they'd be having, not on how perfect they were decidedly *not* for each other.

Not at all.

Chapter Ten

After mere minutes of casually strolling around the town square, he and Cara acquired the target.

A dog-loving woman.

She nudged his shoulder and dropped her voice to a whisper, tipping her forehead to a ponytailed blonde half a block away. "There. At two o'clock on the other side of town square. She just spotted you and Henry. I'll hang back."

"I'll pretend I don't even know you." He winked at her.

"That'll be easy, since I'm about to disappear that-a-way," she said, pointing her thumb at one of the benches on the grass.

As she settled onto the green slats, lowering her shades, he continued walking the feisty pup. Frisky today, Henry pulled hard on the leash, launching himself to the far end of the leather, determined to be the lead man, evidently. "Heel, Henry," he said in a firm tone, then gave a quick tug to pull the tan and white guy back by his side. The dog peered up as if to say, *This good enough for ya?*

Travis bent down to administer a quick pat on the head as Henry panted in the late afternoon heat. "Good boy."

Promptly, the dog darted back ahead, his heel having lasted all of five seconds.

Travis tried again and met the same result.

Damn. Henry was a stubborn boy. Once more he followed Cara's earlier instruction for teaching a dog to heel, tugging him back next to him and praising him, but the dog lunged forward.

Only fifteen pounds, Henry still packed a punch. What he lacked in size, he made up for in pure determination.

"Let's try again," Travis said in an even tone, but as they neared the corner, the target came into range—the blond woman who'd zeroed in on the two of them from across the square was a few feet away. This was the first test of the dog's wingman skills. At the Bachelor Fireman's Auction, Henry would have to be onstage with Travis and the emcee of the event. The dog would need to be on his best behavior to achieve winning dog-and-fireman status. Travis glanced back at Cara, who was perched on the bench, watching, ready to give notes. He wanted to impress her with Henry's quick learning, and Travis hoped the dog could pull this off—

Nails scratched against the sidewalk.

The dog panted loudly.

Then barked happily.

And he made his first attempt to achieve his dog flight wings, launching himself airborne at the blonde.

Wait.

No.

That wasn't his plan at all.

Please, lord. Henry wasn't doing *that,* was he?

But he was. Yes, he was.

Travis grappled at the leash, cringing as he tugged, while Henry wrapped his paws around the woman's leg and went to town humping it, all fifteen pounds of him intent on making puppies with this stranger's bare leg. Travis yanked quickly, freeing her from the unwanted advance. But then the woman stumbled and grabbed hold of the rimmed edge of a garbage can for balance.

He'd have blushed, if he were a blusher. "I'm sorry about that. He's just a puppy," Travis said, offering her a hand and helping her steady herself.

"Perhaps it's time to get him neutered," she said, shaking her finger at the dog, as if Henry understood such admonishments.

"He *is* neutered," Travis muttered as the woman scurried away.

He shrugged, swiveled around, and caught Cara's gaze. She mirrored him, as they both held up their hands in a chorus of *what can you do?*

Travis cut across the emerald green grass of the square as Cara met him in the middle.

"Evidently I'm going to need to change his name to Randy," Travis said, deadpan.

She flashed him a warm smile. "It's okay. We've got two weeks," she said, her voice calm and even. "We'll get him there. He's not going to be perfect the first time. We need to see how he behaves naturally to know what to work on."

"Not quite sure he's a chick magnet. More like the wild humper. Can we call him that on stage?" He affected the deep, warm tones of an announcer. "And now, up for auction is our next bachelor fireman, Travis Jansen, and his dog. You might know him better as...*The Wild Humper,"* he said, then launched into a pretend drum roll.

Cara laughed. "As long as it's not you they're introducing as *The Wild Humper,* I think we'll be okay." She kneeled down to scratch Henry's ears. One ear drooped down, and one popped up. "You're learning how to reel 'em in, right, little fella? But maybe try some cuddling and sweetness first, before you break out the wood."

Henry panted in answer, and somehow almost seemed to be smiling for Cara. Such a flirt, that dog was. A ladies man in training.

Cara rose, held out her hand, and asked for the leash. "Allow the master to show you how it's done," she said, raising an eyebrow and speaking in a pretend-haughty tone.

"Ah, I knew it. You were just setting me up."

She bumped him with her hip. "Yup. Setting a trap. That's my style."

A barely audible groan rumbled through his chest as her body made the barest bit of contact. "Just like you did with me the other night," he said, unable to resist teasing her back. Come to think of it, he was barely able to resist much of anything with her. She had his number; she knew how to play him, from her sexy lingerie ensembles, to her out-of-the-blue challenges, to her boldness in spelling out all her desires. Cara Bailey was sexy, witty, and sweet, all wrapped up in one absolutely delectable package of womanhood. No wonder Henry was making googly eyes at her.

"So I trapped you into having me as a snack on your table?" Cara said, staring down the slope of her nose at him. He wanted to nibble on that nose.

He laughed and shook his head, resisting the powerful

urge to touch her in some way that very second. Draw her in for a kiss. Brush his fingertips across the bare skin of her arm. But they weren't having that kind of fling—the kind where they were allowed to be practitioners of PDA in the middle of their hometown. A hot kiss on a nightclub floor in San Francisco was one thing; a sweet, possessive kiss, as if he were claiming her as his, for the whole town to see, was another. "No. I meant trapped me into something else you know I can't resist. In addition to you, that is."

She furrowed her brow. "What's that?"

"Your car needs a little tinkering."

She swatted him on the arm. "Are you still doing that?"

His eyes went wide. He acted surprised. "Doing what?"

"You are the king of car tinkering. Remember when the headlight went out that night my dad let me borrow his car so we could go bowling?"

He nodded as the memory of one of their dates from years ago resurfaced. The headlight had winked on and off as they drove to the alley, but on the way home, it gasped its last breath. Travis had always been handy, so he fixed it, and her dad had even thanked him profusely for not only bringing his daughter home on time, but for repairing the car. He laughed quietly, remembering how he'd wanted to impress Mr. Bailey, probably because he liked Mr. Bailey's daughter so much and wanted to earn the respect of her dad, too.

"What can I say? I was blessed with the handy genes," he said.

She rolled her eyes. "Indeed you were. So what's wrong with my car that calls for your mad tinkering skills? Since you somehow think I trapped you into fixing it."

"That's a trap I like. Anyway, I noticed the dashboard

lights were pretty dim when I drove it to your house the other night. I think an alternator cable might be loose, but it was dark out and I wasn't able to fix it then."

"So you want to play mechanic with my car?"

"I would very much like to get under your hood," he said with an over-the-top groan, wiggling his eyebrows as she chuckled loudly, clasping a hand on her belly, her pretty laughter sounding like a tinkling bell. Damn, this woman was under his skin. Even the way she laughed made his heart thump a little harder.

What the hell was going on with him? Must be the heat. Yeah, that had to be it. That explained the speed of his heart right now.

"You're on." She tipped her forehead to Henry. "But first, let's get this boy ready for the stage. We've got a mission. Henry and I are going to make sure you raise the money for the firefighter's charity. Right, Henry?"

The dog panted in answer.

Cara turned back to Travis. "Don't worry. I know this is important. I'll do everything I can to help you secure that matching donation."

"Thank you. I really appreciate it," he said, looking her square in the eyes. He hoped his expression conveyed his gratitude for her effort, because he didn't know if he had all the words. Of course, what he really wanted to tell her, too, was how much he liked that he could make dirty comments about wanting to get his hands on her one minute, and then serious ones about a cause that mattered deeply to him the next. She was easy to talk to, and they seemed to move seamlessly from one topic to the next.

"I also have an idea for a special little thing we can have

him do at the end of your stage time."

"Like a trick?"

She nodded. "Exactly. We need to get the basics down first, but if he does well, I have a"—she stopped to noodle on the words—"pièce de résistance, if you will."

"I'm all ears," he said, and she told him her plan.

"Love it. But let's make sure he can walk with me first."

Henry reined in his urges to mate with women's legs, and for the next thirty minutes he was much better at walking in stride next to Travis, though he did growl and lunge at a squirrel who had the audacity to nibble on an apple core in the middle of the sidewalk.

"We're making progress," Cara said with a smile, and for the briefest of seconds he wanted to say *Yes, we are*, as if she'd been talking about the two of them. But she meant the dog, of course.

· · ·

As they walked along the town square on the way to her nearby home, Cara swore Travis was about to hold her hand just outside his mom's bookstore.

"I'll pop in later to say hi to her," he said, nodding to An Open Book. As they strolled past the "Gifts for Grads!" display of *Oh, the Places You'll Go*, she was certain he started to reach out to lace his fingers through hers.

A flicker of a smile worked its way across her lips, and she moved her hand closer.

But then he looped that hand around Henry's leash. In the blink of an eye, she jammed her hands into the pockets of her shorts, as if she were erasing the possibility that had dared to touch down in her mind.

She wished he would hold her hand or drape an arm around her shoulders. She'd always loved his sweet affection in public, as if he'd wanted the world to know she was with him. Maybe he wanted that now, too. True, she didn't harbor any illusions that their fling would extend beyond two weeks, but she couldn't deny how much she thoroughly enjoyed the special little things he did—replacing the stolen biscuits, offering to fix her car, or even his trips down memory lane. They felt *special* and she relished them.

A woman with a sleek bob a few stores up waved to her. Alycia, of the newly trimmed brunette hairdo, was locking up the Silver Pine tasting room for the afternoon.

"Hey, Alycia. The pinot was to die for," Cara said as she stopped to chat briefly.

Alycia beamed. "Excellent. I'm so glad you liked it."

"I enjoyed every single sip."

"I thought it was pretty damn good, too," Travis interjected. Cara glanced at him. His eyes were twinkling; he hadn't touched the wine at his house. He'd simply enjoyed the effect it had had on Cara. The fact that he was making an inside joke had her heart pittering and pattering the slightest bit.

"Even better," Alycia said.

Travis nodded to her storefront, and to the shelves of wines beyond the glass window displays. "Your shelves holding up okay, Alycia?"

She gave a thumbs up. "Perfect. Thank you for fixing them for me. What would I do without the town handyman?" The brunette patted his shoulder in thanks, and a strange burst of jealousy ripped through Cara. She clenched a fist, trying to ignore the unpleasant sensation. It was foolish for Cara to think she was special. Travis didn't do "special." He was straightforward about what he could give a woman, and the things that made her feel special were simply part and parcel of who he was. He was a good guy. He'd helped Alycia. He was about to help Cara with her car. That was good enough.

Case closed.

Alycia flipped her keys up and down in her hand as she peered at Travis, then at Cara, as if she were fitting the puzzle pieces together. "You two together again?"

The resounding *no* tumbled out of both their mouths at the same time. Cara looked at Travis and forced out a laugh. Good thing they both agreed resolutely on that point.

"I'm just training his dog," she answered.

"Of course. Sorry. Looked like you were…" She let her voice trail off, then waved her hand as if she were dismissing a crazy idea. "I need to be on my way. See you around."

As they resumed the walk to her house, Cara filed the encounter in her head as a useful reminder to refrain from superimposing her future dreams and wishes onto a relationship that had a countdown attached to it.

She intended to enjoy every single moment of their brief time together. That was the point of their tryst, after all—to make the most of this time, so she could get him out of her system once and for all.

Chapter Eleven

Minutes later, Cara perched on the edge of her dryer in the garage, kicking her foot absently back and forth as she enjoyed the view.

She tilted her head to the side, considering the damn near perfect sight in front of her. She couldn't decide what was the best part of the scene.

On the one hand, there was that sexy sliver of his back that showed as his white T-shirt rode up.

On the other hand, there was that succulent ass. His jeans hugged his butt so perfectly that all she wanted to do was squeeze those cheeks.

And then there were his arms, and they were pretty damn spectacular too, all lean and corded, ripped with trim muscles as he worked his magic on her little car.

Yup, she could do a damn fine job fixating on the physical. She'd shoved all her wandering thoughts of holding hands and being special straight into a cupboard and slammed the door on them. The countdown was ticking, and every second should be a sexy one. That was the *only* way she was ever going to expunge Travis from the real estate he'd claimed in her head—by objectifying him.

"Almost done," he said, fiddling with some wires under the hood. Damn, he was hot when he was handy. There was just something about a man who could fix things, something that turned her on high and sent a charge of heat through her body.

"I could have done it in one minute," she said, teasing him because it hadn't taken him long at all. A minute or two, tops.

He turned around and narrowed his eyes. "Oh, yeah? You can fix a car?"

She scoffed and waved her hand in the air. "Absolutely." She *was* handy enough; her father had taught her a few basics of auto maintenance.

"Yeah, right."

"Actually, I know a few things. But I'd just rather not deal with it. Play to your strengths and all. So I'm really glad you're helping," she said, stripping the teasing from her tone. She was completely earnest now—just because she had mastered a few basic DIY skills didn't mean she enjoyed puttering around the house or the engine.

"I feel the same way about cooking. I can do it. I'd just rather not," he said as he finished, turned around, and held out his arms wide, presenting her with a fixed car. "There you go."

She hopped off the dryer and wrapped her arms around his neck. She saw no reason to hold back in private, especially since her body was longing to be close to him. She hated that she had someplace else to be soon because all she wanted was...*him*. She planted a quick kiss on his lips, then patted the hood. "Thank you. I've got an appointment with another client at six, so I'm glad to know everything is working perfectly."

His lips curved down, disappointment etched in his features. "Too bad. Because I was really hoping we were going to act out your fantasy from the other night. I've been waiting to hear what helped you sleep."

A shiver ran down her spine. Admittedly, she'd been wanting that, too. Desperately. While there might not be time for all she craved, there was always time for a little something. She jutted up her shoulder provocatively, the move letting her tank top strap slide closer to her arm. "Why do you assume we can't?"

"Maybe because you just said you had to go," he said, his eyes now tracking the bare skin of her shoulder.

"I do need to go," she said, trailing her fingers down his chest, across his abs, and to the waistband of his jeans. "But I'm pretty sure we can fit this in. I'm going to need you to close the hood on my car to do this right, though."

He raised an eyebrow approvingly, as he closed the hood, letting it slam shut. "So your fantasy involves you, me, and the car?"

"Perhaps it does."

He held up his hands to show the grease on them. "Just a second. Need to wash up so I don't cover you in grease. Though, let the record reflect, you'd look completely hot as an auto mechanic, and I'd never take my truck to anyone but you, even if you put the headlights on the tires."

She laughed as he headed inside to wash his hands at the

kitchen sink. Henry was hanging out in the house with her dog. When Travis returned, freshly scrubbed, he parked his hands on his hips. "So what's it gonna be?"

"You. Hood of my car. Now."

He groaned in appreciation. "I do believe this might be something I've been thinking of, too."

"Oh have you?" She walked closer, giving him a tap on his chest. He pretended it was hard enough to launch him back onto the hood.

"Possibly."

"What do you think it is?" She climbed on him, straddling him on the green hood of her Mini Cooper, pinning him under her.

"Something that involves this, maybe," he said, then brushed his fingertip across her top lip. She drew it into her mouth and sucked—a long, luxurious, decadent stroke.

His eyes rolled back into his head.

He breathed out hard as she swirled her tongue along his finger.

His lips parted, but no words came out, and she thrilled that this simple act was enough of a turn-on to render this man speechless. She couldn't wait to wrap her lips around him, even though that wasn't the fantasy she'd gotten off to the other night. But it was still one of her many dirty thoughts about him, so she wasn't going to object to taking him into her mouth right now. Judging from the hard ridge of his cock pressed against her thigh through his jeans, he wasn't going to protest one bit either.

As she sucked his finger, her hands traveled along the white cotton of his shirt. When she reached the waistband, she let go of his finger and pushed up his shirt to reveal his fantastically hard chest and carved abs. He pulled it over his head and tossed it on the hood.

"Now I get to admire you," she said with a happy sigh, as she gazed at his gorgeous body—her playground for another week or so. Her real estate. Her temporary, gorgeous, handy, dog-loving man.

She danced her fingers across the hard ladder of his abdomen.

"I'm liking your fantasies," he said, his voice rough and hungry. "Especially if they start like this."

He took charge, grabbing the back of her head and pulling her close for a searing kiss, consuming her lips, claiming her mouth, and making her dizzy with lust. His lips were soft and he kissed like a fevered dream, hot and sultry, the kind of dream that made you wake up in a sweat. That made you ache between your legs. That consumed you with want. That's how he kissed her—like it was some kind of exquisite surrender to kissing, even in her garage, even on the hood of her car.

Maybe that was why he was the one guy she couldn't get out of her system. Because they didn't need romantic backdrops. They didn't require sunsets or summer rains for a kiss to be spectacular. They didn't need moonlight or shooting stars. He kissed her like a shooting star, leaving a bright burning path across the midnight sky, as his fingers grappled with her hair, and his lips owned hers.

She ground against him, rubbing against his rock hard cock until he groaned so loudly he broke the kiss.

She clasped his face in her hands and stared him in the eyes. "I want to do other things with my lips now," she said, and he pushed up against her, his steel length making her damp between her legs.

His eyes blazed darkly, the hungry look in them making her heart pump wildly with need for him. She bent her head to his neck, brushing her lips across his stubbled jaw as her chest pressed to his. "I'm going to suck your dick so good," she whispered, half shocked and half thrilled that he brought out this naughty, dirty side in her.

"*Now.* I'm dying for you, now," he said as he pushed her shoulders, guiding her down, down, down his body.

She unzipped his jeans. Her breath stilled as she gazed at the bulge in his black boxer briefs, savoring the outline of his erection. She'd seen him before, she'd tasted him, she knew the feel of his cock. But still, she wanted to relish every second of this unveiling of his hard length. She tugged his jeans down to his knees, then his briefs, and his erection sprang free.

Thick. Long. Beautiful.

Her mouth watered. She wanted him. In her. On her. Everywhere. Her hand wrapped around his dick, satiny smooth to the touch and hard and throbbing in her palm.

"I bet I can make you come in less than five minutes."

. . .

Two minutes was more like it, given where his thoughts had been all day. All week. All year.

Hell, she'd made him come many times in his shower, or late at night in his bed when he took matters into his own hands. He'd jacked off to the image of her more times than he'd ever admit because he knew the wonders of her wicked tongue. He'd taught her how to give a blow job way back when—though *taught* wasn't quite the right word. She'd asked him one night when they were teenagers to show him how he liked it, and he'd gladly obliged that request.

"Can I lay my bets on—" But the rest of his sentence was swallowed up in a growl as she wrapped her lips around the head of his dick, licking and swirling her tongue across him.

His eyed raked over her, imprinting the sexy pose she was in, her knees digging into the metal of the hood, her hair spilling across his thighs. One hand was pressed on the hood, the other was wrapped tightly around the base of his cock, stroking him as she sucked.

"That's perfect," he rasped out as he rocked into her mouth. She sucked harder, deeper, the head hitting the back of her throat. She wasted no time with teasing him. She went straight to work, moving this blow job up the scale quickly from a teasing tongue to full-on friction.

He drew a deep inhalation then traced her lips with his fingertip as she sucked. "Love that," he murmured. "Love those lips. I love how sweet and pretty they look when you smile, but how sinful they are on me. Is this what you got off to the other night?"

She shrugged in a flirty way, briefly meeting his gaze.

"I've gotten off to this so many times. I fucking love the way you look right now," he said, pleasure ripping through him as his eyes roamed her from head to toe, and the way she made it a full body blow job—moving her hips, rocking her mouth, and having a field day with her tongue and lips. Heat sizzled through his veins as she wrapped her lips so tightly around him there was no goddamn give between her mouth and his shaft.

This was blow job heaven.

A groan escaped his throat.

Loud. Guttural. Animalistic.

The friction was intense, all tight, hot suction that had desire climbing up his spine, ratcheting higher and higher with each wicked stroke, each tantalizing lick. He dragged his fingers through her hair, pushing it away from her face so he could get a perfect view of her lips sucking his dick. "I'm imagining you on your bed, trying to fall asleep, but still all hot and wet, and your fingers start stroking yourself while you're picturing taking me in your mouth."

Her eyes glittered darkly at him, like she was saying that was exactly what she'd done.

She flattened her tongue on a down stroke, hitting him with such pleasure it was like a current surging through his skin. She took her hand off him and dropped it between her own legs.

"Oh god," he groaned, losing words, losing thought, losing track of everything but the rush of watching her slide her fingers inside her shorts at the same time she took him deep.

"*Cara,*" he moaned, his eyes squeezing shut as the world blurred. His body jolted with each warm thrust of her mouth, as visions flashed before him—of her pleasure, her orgasms, her lush, sexy body that he wanted more than any man had a right to want a woman. He succumbed to the intensity tearing through his bloodstream, as his hands darted out to spear her hair, curling through the strands. "I'm coming," he whispered, and then white heat exploded behind his eyes as his body detonated.

The pleasure rode over him in waves, like a tsunami,

crashing, roaring, smashing into him. Taking him under.

A minute later, she was crawling up next to him, sliding alongside him, wedging her body next to his. Instantly, he wrapped his arms around her and tugged her in close. He wasn't sure where the impulse to hold her tight after a blow job that torched his brain to smithereens came from, but there it was. He wanted nothing more than to have her in his arms, hear her heart beat against his chest, feel the whisper of her breath on his skin.

Well, he did want something more. He wanted all of her.

"What time is your appointment?"

"Ten minutes. I need to go," she said.

He groaned, jamming a hand through his hair as he sat and pulled up his briefs and pants. "Why do we have the worst timing?"

"I don't know that our timing is so bad. That was less than three minutes, so I'd say it was pretty good timing."

He laughed. "I give you all the credit for rocking my world. I don't even want to ask where you learned how to give a blow job like that."

She swatted him. "Yeah, you don't need to ask because you know," she said, then scooted off him. "I need to go freshen up. But thank you for fixing my car. Since you don't like to cook, maybe I can make you dinner to say thank you."

"You don't have to do anything to say thank you, but I'll happily take dinner. Because I like food, and I like you," he said, those last words slipping out in a tender voice that surprised him. Maybe it surprised her, too, because her breath seemed to catch momentarily.

He didn't want to use that voice. That voice meant closeness. It meant *more*. They were having none of those things.

They were simply having fun, so he recalibrated to focus on that. On the sex, and the elimination of distractions on the path to the sex. "What do you think about making sure we have no interruptions next time? Like making a date. Maybe a dinner date. Here at your house."

She smiled, so wide and so bright that his heart tripped over itself. This damn heart was becoming a problem, too. He'd need to give it a talking-to later, and tell it to calm the fuck down around her.

"I would like that very much," she said. "I have to drop some items off at the Sonoma animal rescue tomorrow afternoon and then I teach an agility class, but the next night is good."

"That's where I got Henry from. I'm supposed to send in his proof of vaccinations, so they know I'm being a good pet owner. Maybe I could drive you down there?"

"That sounds great. And, when we have dinner you should bring Henry to my house. He can hang out with Violet as we dine. Oh, and by the way, I wasn't thinking about blowing you when I got off to you the other night."

He arched an eyebrow. "You weren't?"

She stepped closer, curled her hand through his hair. "I have this fantasy about walking in on you when you're getting off to me."

His eyes widened. They nearly popped out of his head. "Are you kidding me?"

She shook her head, a naughty grin spreading on her face. "I'm not kidding. I have this fantasy that it's dark, I walk in and I find you in your bed or maybe the shower, totally unaware that I'm watching you as you pleasure your-self. And you're picturing me. Your eyes are closed, and your hand is working yourself over, and you're beyond aroused because you're thinking of me. And I just find you like that. You open your eyes, and I tell you to finish, and you do, watching me the whole time like you want to eat me up."

His dick rose to a mile high again. "Come by my house late one night and you're bound to find that. I think about you so much, Cara. So fucking much. You are the sexiest, prettiest woman I've ever known." He cupped her shoulders and looked her in the eyes, so she would know he meant every word. "And I'm glad you wanted to have this last fling with me."

Her smile erased itself with that word. She dropped her hand from his hair.

"I mean, because it's fun," he added, as if he needed to explain.

She nodded, her lips fixed in a ruler-straight line as she spoke. "Totally fun. That was the point. Getting you out of my system, like we're doing."

"And it's working?"

"Absolutely."

But as she turned to go and he gathered up his dog, he wondered why she'd seemed so cold when he said *last fling*.

That was what this was, right? There was no way it could be anything else.

Chapter Twelve

The faded, lemon yellow THANKS FOR VISITING HIDDEN OAKS sign loomed a few hundred feet ahead of them—a weather-worn, oversize wooden billboard on the corner of the winding two-lane highway that escorted them out of town.

"Did you miss Hidden Oaks when you lived in San Francisco?" Travis asked as he drove along the curvy, concrete ribbon that cut through the rolling emerald green hills of the county. The blankets, towels, leashes, and collars that she'd collected to help animals in need—from clients and in partnership with the fancy dog store off the town square—were in the bed of his truck.

Briefly, she reflected on his question. Life was different here than in the city. There were benefits to both, but she knew where her heart lay. "I did enjoy all the restaurants, and the bike paths along the Bay are great for walking dogs. But it's hard for me *not* to miss this town. I love it here, which probably explains why I came back a lot to visit my parents and my sisters."

"You're close with your sisters." He said it as a fact, and she liked that he knew this about her. She was about to ask if he remembered Stacy quizzing him about his intentions on prom night, but she didn't have to because he kept speaking. "Remember when Stacy opened the door on prom night, and pretty much grilled me about taking you out? First time I ever met her."

Cara laughed as she lowered her window to let in some fresh air. "She gave you the third degree and then some."

"I expected to find your father at the door. But there was the big sister instead, with a stern look on her face. I think we had just started dating a few weeks before and they didn't really know me."

"You'd already proven yourself to my father by fixing the car, and winning him over that way. But you had to pass the sister test, too. Good thing Sofie was still in college or she could have made you jump through hoops."

He slowed the truck as the light ahead turned red. "Stacy was so scary then. She had her hands on her hips, and her face was all serious, and she asked what time I intended to bring you home."

She leaned in close and whispered conspiratorially. "Guess we tricked them when we answered that question."

He smiled slyly. "Yes, we did."

Cara laughed, smacking the windowsill with the memory. She'd told Stacy and her parents that she was sleeping over at a friend's house, and instead, she and Travis spent the night in a tent on the trails at the end of Miner's Road.

"Stacy was working in Calistoga at the time. Did you know she came over that night just to decide if she approved of you?" Cara said, as the light changed and they drove on, passing lush acres of vines, rich with row upon row of grapes opening up to the warm sun.

"Did she? Approve of me?"

"She let me go out with you, didn't she?" Cara said, raising an eyebrow. "She's a protective big sister. She's let up a bit now that she has her own kids, but she still looks out for me."

"And does she still have to approve of your dates?" he said in a teasing tone.

"Of course," Cara said, with a straight face. "She comes over before every single one."

Travis glanced away from the road, his eyes dark and intense. "Actually, let's not talk about dates you're going on," he said through gritted teeth, a clear note of jealousy seeping into his tone.

"You sure you don't want to hear about the checklist she has for me?" Cara said, egging him on. She kind of liked this side of him—the side that didn't want to hear a word about other men.

"No," he said sharply.

"Not even a teeny, tiny bit?"

He huffed out a frustrated sigh. "Fine. What's her checklist?"

She drummed her fingers on the console, as if making a big pronouncement. Then she spoke her own truth. "Clever, kind, good with kids, good with animals, and treats me well," she said, keeping her eyes on him the whole time as she listed her own traits. Stacy didn't truly have a checklist. All Stacy wanted was for her little sister to be happy, and Cara knew what her own heart needed to get there—those five things.

Keeping one hand on the wheel, he stole a glance, then brushed a strand of her hair off her shoulders. "That's what you deserve," he said softly. The jealousy had vacated, but there was a wistfulness in his tone now, and that new sound possessed a faint echo of disappointment.

She wasn't so sure she wanted to linger in this strange zone of what they were and what they would never be. She changed gears, as if she were taking a sharp right to a new route. "What about you?"

He furrowed his brow, shooting her a quizzical look. "Do I have a checklist?"

She laughed lightly. "No. I meant—did you miss Hidden Oaks when you were gone? For college," she said, prompting him. "That was the only time you were away from here, right?"

After their brief summer romance, he'd left for school in Southern California, while she'd gone to college locally.

"I did miss it here. Don't get me wrong—I enjoyed college immensely, and the chance to get away. But Megan had just started high school when I left, so I tried to come back as often as I could to check in on her," he said, clicking on the turn signal as they neared the road with the shelter. He cast his gaze briefly to Cara, then back to the road. "And I missed you when I left."

She sat up higher and jerked her head to stare at him. That had been the last thing she'd expected him to say. They'd both tried so hard then to be cool about their inevitable end. They'd aimed to be smart and sophisticated and to go into their brief summer romance with eyes wide open, knowing it would end of its own accord. Neither had ever voiced the possibility of missing each other. They'd been so purposefully tough, even though they were only eighteen.

"You did?" she asked cautiously, in a tentative breath.

"Of course. I was crazy about you. You know that," he said, speaking as if his feelings then were a matter of public record. Yes, he had said as much to her that summer, and those words—*crazy for you*—set off sparklers in her heart at the time. Now, more than a decade later, they were no less potent, and they sent a thrill through her bloodstream.

Then, as quickly as the conversation had taken this unexpected turn, it swerved back. "So that answers your question if I missed Hidden Oaks. I guess you can't keep me out of this town. I'm just a small town boy," he said, singing the last few lines to the tune of the Journey song with similar opening lyrics—*Just a small town girl.*

Cara rustled in her purse, and in seconds, she'd called up "Don't Stop Believing" on her phone. She hit play. "Sing it with me."

"You're crazy," he said, shaking his head as he laughed.

"C'mon. You're a good car singer. Do it."

"Nah. I can't sing and drive."

She squeezed his thigh. "Yes. You can. C'mon, Travis. Sing," she said, bumping her shoulder against his as the melody built.

She didn't know why it was so important that he did, but she didn't plan to let up 'til he was singing his heart out with her.

• • •

He was only giving her a hard time for the sake of giving her a hard time. He didn't mind singing along at all. It certainly wasn't something he did with the guys, but Cara had her sexy, flirty, sweet way of bringing out these other sides of him. As she turned up the volume on her phone, blasting the song, he belted it out for the final few miles until they pulled into the lot at the shelter.

When the song finished, she stabbed the end button on the playlist with a flourish. "There you go. We rocked it."

"We sure know how to have a good time."

She flashed him the prettiest smile he'd ever seen. "We do. We are making the most of our brief fling, aren't we?"

"We are," he said as he opened the door. He wasn't surprised he was having so much fun with her. The time he'd spent with her years ago contained some of his happiest memories, and their prior summer romance was the closest he'd ever come to truly falling for a woman.

Good thing they'd had an end in sight then, and good thing they did now, too. Nobody got hurt that way.

They both knew the score.

They headed into the animal shelter to hand over the blankets and towels for the animals, and to give the manager the final paperwork for his dog.

"I'm glad to hear everything is going great with Henry," the shelter manager said, waving good-bye as they walked out.

As Travis opened the door to his truck for her, Cara glanced at her watch, reminding him she had a class to teach.

"What time is your agility session?" he asked.

"I've got an hour. It should probably take about twenty minutes to get there though, so I have a little extra time."

An idea landed in his head as he walked around to his

side and got in. "Remember yesterday when you mentioned our nearly disastrous bowling date? The alley is on the way back. We could stop in for a quick game."

She crinkled her nose. "I don't know if there's enough time for a game."

"Okay, so how about we play whoever gets the most points in thirty minutes? That should give you time to get to your class."

She didn't answer right away. Instead, her blue eyes seemed to twinkle with mischief as he turned the key in the ignition. "What if I win? Are you going to wash my car like you did Smith's?" she asked, and he laughed at the reminder.

"You want me to? If that's what you want I'll gladly do it."

She narrowed her eyes, and pursed her lips, feigning intense concentration. "Let's make the bet for something else. If I win the most points, you are going to bake some of your sister's amazing chocolate chip cookies for me for tomorrow night."

"Fair enough," he said with a nod. "And if I win?"

"Well, what do you want?" she asked, leaning in closer to him, invitingly.

That was the easiest thing in the world to answer. He ran his hand along her thigh. "For you to not wear underwear when I show up at your door tomorrow night."

She held out a hand to shake. "It's on."

He took her hand, tugged her in close, and dropped a kiss on her gorgeous mouth. He'd intended for it to be a quick kiss, so they could be on their way. But the taste of her lips was too delicious. He kissed her deeply, their mouths crashing together, their tongues tangling, the heat between them rising. He could have kissed her for so much longer, could have pulled into a parking spot around the back of the shelter and gone for more. But he wanted to have his way with her completely, no clock ticking, no deadlines, nothing but her.

He especially wanted to win their bowling bet.

Badly.

But a half hour later, as he drove her to her agility class, she tap-danced her fingers across his jeans. "I cannot wait for those cookies."

Chapter Thirteen

Travis extended a hand to one of his longtime clients. The beak-nosed, beanpole venture capitalist clasped it and shook heartily.

"You did well. You paced yourself," Travis said, pleased that Hunter had started to rein in his overly aggressive style.

"Wasn't easy. I was dying to bet it all on that one hand," Hunter said, shaking his head as if he were amazed he'd held back. The air-conditioning hummed softly in the background of the upscale private club in San Francisco, one of those members-only type of places.

Hell, Travis was amazed at Hunter's self-control when he'd had two jacks. Playing that hand wisely had helped him to win. "That's what I'm talking about. More of that. Keep doing *that*. Got it?" he said, letting go of Hunter's palm and heading to the door of the suite.

"Got it, boss," Hunter said with a salute. "I have a game in Napa in two weeks, but don't worry. I know you've got your bachelor auction that weekend anyway. Maybe I'll even bid on you and help you win for that charity of yours."

Travis laughed. "Please don't bid on me."

"Just kidding. Anyway, I might not even need you to help me prep for the game."

Travis smiled. "Nothing could please me more. My goal is to make you so good that you don't need me. If I do that, I've done my job."

"I love that your mission is obsolescence."

That hadn't been easy with this man. Hunter loved to bet, loved to go all in—probably why he remained Travis's top client. He needed Travis because risks were too alluring for him—hence Travis still being here, several years later, walking him through his games. Hunter ran a poker tournament once a month at this club, as well as regular weekly games with his wealthy Silicon Valley buddies.

"I'm going to hit the road," Travis said, and quickly covered the miles between the city and Hidden Oaks. He stopped at the grocery store, picked up some items for that night, and quickly set to work in the kitchen when he arrived home. Then he showered, and dressed for his dinner date.

He buttoned up the final buttons on the crisp white shirt, combed his hair, and brushed his teeth. He flashed a quick smile in the mirror to inspect his teeth. Not that he'd have anything stuck between them—he hadn't eaten since a lunch break at the game earlier that day.

The game had been civilized and drew a clean-cut business crowd. Those were Hunter's rules, and he'd set them up because he'd unknowingly dabbled in some rigged games a while ago. Hunter invited him to play occasionally, too, knowing it would up the game to play with someone like

Travis—someone who had taught them when to hold, when to fold, and when to go all in. Travis wasn't some poker god, with aspirations for the Texas Hold 'Em TV circuit, nor did he long to march through Vegas casinos, mopping up chips like a king. But he had the requisite pro cred, and he also had a knack for the game.

He played like he fought fires. He knew how to read a fire, and he knew how to read the players in a game. He was calculating, he assessed the situation, and he'd learned to pick the best route through the tough spots, just like a fire. Detect the hot zones. Check the door temperature before opening it. Spray water on a surface to see if it sizzles. Didn't always beat the fire, and didn't always win a hand, but the strategy had proven successful over time in both fields. He'd honed his card skills thanks to his firehouse mentor—the guy who'd looked after Travis when his dad was gone, who'd taught him both the card game and how to battle a blaze.

Today's game had required steady focus and a cool hand, because the other venture capitalists Hunter brought in were used to taking big risks.

That was where Travis was different. He'd spent his lifetime taking necessary precautions, practicing safety, determining how near or how far to push. The approach had served him well, and today he returned home with a few hundred extra bucks that went straight to the bank.

Well, some of it went to the Families of Fallen Firefighters. The charity had sent out another email to its supporters that afternoon, asking for help, citing the downswing in giving in the last few years, which had hit it hard and led to cuts in support services. Travis had responded immediately, donating as much as he could part with from his winnings.

But the email had made his shoulders tense as a kernel of anxiety sped through him. He *had* to win the auction. He desperately wanted to be one of the reasons the charity could keep doing its good work. Win the auction, snag the matching grant from the insurance broker, and help send the Families of Fallen Firefighters back on the upswing. That was the mission.

And then, a bit of his earnings from today made their way to the grocery store, because he'd picked up butter, chocolate chips, brown sugar, and the other ingredients to bake the cookies for Cara. These chocolate chip cookies were pretty much the pinnacle of culinary delight, and it had made perfect sense that Cara wanted to win them.

He snapped his fingers. Megan had something else he knew Cara would like.

He rolled up the cuffs on his shirt, headed to the kitchen to grab the Tupperware container full of cookies, and tucked his phone to his ear as he dialed his sister and made his request.

"Come on by," she said. "Becker's at the bar, and it's just me here right now, so you won't have to be embarrassed by him teasing you."

"Whew. 'Cause I don't need shit from him right now."

"You'll only get it from me. See you soon," she said, but her voice sounded muted and she hung up quicker than usual.

He shrugged to himself. He'd be seeing her soon enough, and if something was wrong, he'd find out. He leashed up Henry and went on his way. When Travis arrived at her house—the one she shared with Becker since she'd moved in with him—he spotted what he wanted by the front porch.

Megan had a green thumb, and a talent for turning any place she lived into a garden paradise. She'd quickly made her mark on Becker's home. His front yard dazzled with a veritable potpourri of vibrant colors—bright orange dahlias, rich purple asters, and sunshine-loving daisies.

He rolled down the window for Henry, who hung his snout out and watched from the passenger seat as Travis walked to the door. He knocked. Becker opened the door. Travis jerked his head, surprised to see his friend. "Hey. I thought you were at The Panting Dog tonight."

"I was. But I came home for a minute," he said.

Travis held up his hands as stop signs. "No need to say more," he said because clearly a *minute* was code for a quickie.

Becker rolled his eyes. "Whatever, man. Megan said you need some flowers."

"I do," he muttered, and wished his sister had answered the door. He didn't need to be harassed by one of the guys about picking up some of Megan's homegrown flowers for a bouquet for the woman he wasn't even truly dating.

Becker slapped a pair of gardening scissors in Travis's hand. "Megan said to take what you want, but be sure to put them in water, so I'll get you a vase."

He furrowed his brow. "Is she okay?"

Becker nodded but said nothing more.

"You sure?"

Another nod was Becker's only answer.

His silence gave Travis pause, especially since Megan hadn't been herself on the phone. But he'd have to trust Becker on this count. "If you say so," Travis said, then he turned and walked down the steps to the front yard. As he snipped a few daisies, his spine tingled with awareness. He looked up. Becker leaned against the side of the house, ankles crossed, arms folded over his chest, a knowing smirk on his face.

"What are you smiling at?"

"You. Bringing flowers to Cara. It kills me," he said, chuckling.

Travis sliced a few asters, keeping his face down, trying to reveal nothing. "How do you know they're for Cara?"

Becker laughed deeply, the sound echoing across the yard. "Oh, that's a good one, Trav. Here's your answer—because I have eyes."

Travis called on his poker skills. He bluffed, mustering his best nonchalant tone. "Just getting them for my mom."

But as the white lie tumbled out, he cringed. What was wrong with him? That was the worst bluff he'd ever attempted.

Becker called him on it. "You let Mrs. Jansen know I hope she enjoys the daisies. I look forward to seeing them on her kitchen table when we stop by tomorrow to have dinner with her," he said, his eyes sparkling with amusement.

Travis rose and held out his hands, full of flowers and scissors. "Fine. You got me. They're for Cara. I'm having dinner with her tonight."

Becker nodded, seemingly satisfied that he'd succeeded in this round. But he pressed on. "Why can't you just admit you're crazy for her?"

Travis narrowed his eyes, a lick of annoyance racing through his blood. He wasn't crazy for her. He wasn't crazy for anyone. "It's just dinner. She's helping me with Henry, that's all. And I helped her with her car," he said, because at least that was all truthful. He was playing these cards better, so he upped the ante of his denial. "And why do you even want me to be crazy for her? You want me to join you on this side? C'mon. You were like me. You stayed out of the line of fire when it came to this stuff."

"Yeah, and then everything changed when I met Megan, and I haven't once looked back. But the funny thing is, man, you look an awful lot like me when I was chasing your sister," he said, gesturing to the burst of color Travis gripped in his palm. "Granted, I've only known you for two years, but never in that time have I seen you bring flowers to a woman."

Travis held his chin high. "I've given plenty of gifts to women before, thank you very much. I'm not some jackass who doesn't do the basics like flowers and chocolate."

Becker laughed. "Fair enough. But from your sister's garden? The flowers your sister grows? That's a horse of a different color. Next you're going to tell me you're baking brownies and cookies for her."

Oh shit. A flush of heat spread over his cheeks. What the hell? He didn't blush. He had no tells. And *now* was the time that a splash of red raced across his face? His brain cycled through possible denials, reaching for something plausible. But he was saved by the appearance of Megan in the doorway. She held out a vase filled with water. Her face looked pale, and her hand felt clammy as he took the vase. "You okay? You don't look so hot."

"I don't feel so hot. I'm a little under the weather," she said, then absently dropped her hand to her belly.

Travis's radar went off, blaring like a police siren. His eyes widened and his jaw went slack. He pointed. "You're pregnant."

Megan's answer flashed in her eyes—a flicker of joy. Her lips dared to curve up ever so briefly with the start of a wild grin that she quickly reined in. "Why would you say that?"

"Who's in denial now?" he said, smiling widely. "I say it because it's true. Isn't it?" He stared hard at her, giving her a look as if he had X-ray vision, knowing it had worked when they were younger. Her lips twitched, and her eyes sparkled, and after a few seconds, she nodded vigorously.

Travis wrapped his arms around his sister, giving her a warm hug. The strangest burst of panic skipped through his nervous system for a second. Everyone he knew was marching forward so purposefully—settling down and starting families. "I'm so happy for you," he said. Even if he was odd man out by personal choice, he was downright thrilled for Megan.

"Thank you," she said softly, choking back a sob.

He pulled back to look her in the eyes. "You're going to be a great mom."

She punched his arm. "You'll be a great uncle."

He turned to Becker, who beamed with pride and happiness. "That's why I found your sorry ass here when you were supposed to be working."

Becker shrugged happily. "Gotta take care of my woman when she's not feeling well. She's the mother of my child soon."

Travis hugged Megan once more. "I guess this means you'll be a pregnant bride."

When he let go, she laughed lightly. "That's fine by me. We weren't trying to prevent it, if you know what I mean."

He laughed. "How far along are you? Have you told Mom?"

"Twelve weeks, and not yet. But I will tomorrow."

Travis mimed zipping his lips. He clapped Becker on the back. "Congratulations, man. I'm unbelievably happy for the two of you. You take good care of her, you hear?" he said, wagging his index finger at his sister's fiancé.

Becker saluted him. "I always do," he said, then draped his arm around Megan and dropped a kiss on her forehead. She beamed at him, and in that wink of a second Travis saw so much love, so much joy, and so much certainty between the two of them. They hadn't even waited to get married; they simply knew they wanted to have a family.

As he drove to Cara's, he did his best to push that warm fuzzy feeling in his chest far away. Those kinds of plans might be perfect for his sister and her man, but they had no place in his life. Not when he'd assessed the risks, and determined the best course of action. That route to safety remained the same—steer clear of serious relationships. They were fraught with too much danger.

He flashed back on a fire he and Becker had fought a few months ago in an old winery, and how the beast of a blaze had tried to eat them alive in a mad dash to scorch everything in its path. Careful and methodical, they'd battled back and took it down, but at any moment things could have gone differently. A fallen beam here, a backdraft there. Take all the precautions in the world, find the hot zones, and you still never knew if your life was about to turn into a blank slate of sadness for years, like his mom's had when his dad left this earth.

Travis prided himself on weighing the options and choosing wisely, on knowing when to act and when to refrain. This situation with Cara was no different. He'd keep his cards close to the vest, only playing the ones that were guaranteed to win.

Like the ace of their chemistry, so to speak.

That was all she wanted from him anyway. There was no need to even worry about the crazy notions Becker had tried to plant in his head.

When he arrived at her house, he had the tin of cookies and Henry's leash in one hand, the vase of flowers in the other, and condoms in his back pocket, a reminder of the type of game he and Cara were playing.

Focus on the sex, he reminded himself.

Besides, it was high time for him to take a dose of her medicine. She was a smart woman, and she knew the cure for what ailed her. He suffered from the same affliction, so he'd take the same remedy and fuck her out of his system too. Take her, have her, claim her.

Then he could finally be free of this hold she had on him. He could stop thinking about her all the damn time, once they finished this brief affair in another week.

When she opened the door, he knew he'd have no problem with his plan. She wore a white sundress that landed mid-thigh, her hair was swept up in a clip, with loose strands framing her beautiful face, and her legs were bare.

In seconds they'd be wrapped around him.

"Hi," she said, her voice sexy sweet.

"Hi."

Henry chimed in next, barking at Violet, who pawed at the floor, eager to play with a four-legged friend.

"I'll let them into the yard and they can chase each other out there," Cara said, then patted the side of her leg, a signal for the dogs to follow her as she walked to the sliding glass door. His eyes stayed on her the whole time, on the white fabric of her dress, the way it fell loosely on her body, and the tantalizing question of whether she was wearing anything under it.

He set the tin of cookies and the flowers on the entryway table and shut the door behind him.

When she returned, he cupped her face in his hands, backed her up against the wall, and kissed her hard and fiercely—so hard all thoughts drained from his head as she speared her hands in his hair, wrapped a leg around his, and kissed him back like she wanted all the same things.

Chapter Fourteen

This was the only way to be kissed—pinned to the wall, bodies coiled together, his lips claiming hers. She was at his mercy, and she willingly gave herself to him. He kissed her like she was his oxygen, like the very thought of not kissing her was hell on earth.

He loosened her hair, tossing the clip on the floor and letting all her black and red strands tumble free. He laced his hands through her hair, curling his fingers around her head.

Her knees weakened, and her stomach practiced swan dives from epic heights. As his lips devoured hers, the temperature inside her shot to nuclear. She melted everywhere from this kiss. From his hands in her hair, to the insistent press of his mouth, to his hard length against her belly, they connected on a primal level where language was wholly unnecessary. Their bodies spoke, saying how much they needed each other.

More than could be measured.

The kiss was delirious; it was white-hot and furious. He kissed her so hard their teeth clicked. They were wild and desperate, crashing into each other in a beautiful collision of lips, tongues, and bodies. She wanted more of this savage kissing, this intense need for another person, so deep, so consuming it could barely be quenched.

This was a kiss that could only end one way.

In toe-curling, shout-to-the-heavens sex.

Oh, how she wanted him. How she wanted him to sink so deep inside her that she saw stars and sang arias.

She found the will to somehow break the kiss. Placing her hands on his chest, she voiced a pure plea. "Now. I want you now. I can't wait any more."

He let go of her hair and pressed his forehead to hers. "I'm going to fuck you now, Cara. I'm going to fuck you like you wanted that night at the club. Like you wanted in my kitchen. Like you wanted on the hood of your car. Because I wanted you so goddamn much all those times, too. I've wanted you every time I've been with you. So much it drives me crazy," he said, his voice hot and rough, his words setting every nerve in her body on fire.

He trailed his hands down her bare arms, reaching the hem of her skirt. Her breath fled her chest from his touch. "Anything on under this sexy little dress?"

"Find out," she said.

He pushed up the fabric, revealing her bare flesh. His chest rose and fell as he stared at her nudity. "I thought I lost the game."

"You did. But I guess you won anyway."

"I did. Because these are my favorite panties," he rasped out, as he drew a finger through her wetness. She trembled in his arms, her body craving more.

"You like tonight's lingerie?"

"I love it," he said, as if each word was succulent. "God, I'm finally going to have you again." His inky blue eyes fixed on her, unwavering. His pupils were dilated, giving away his desire for her. Though, everything about him revealed his need. She heard it in his words, and she *knew* it in his touch, in his gaze, in the intensity that radiated off him. She'd never felt so wanted.

"Do you have a condom?" she whispered, her throat crackling with dryness.

He nodded. "Hell yeah."

As he reached into his back pocket, she made fast work of unbuttoning his shirt, thrilling at the feel of his chest against her hands. She could explore that chest forever, map him with her fingertips, study him and never grow tired of his body, or of the way he responded to her touch. Like she was the only woman he'd ever wanted like this.

"Take me now, please take me now," she said, fumbling at his jeans, unbuttoning then unzipping. She couldn't wait any longer. She was ready to rip the condom packet out of his hand because he was taking so long to open it, precise and methodical as he carefully tore the foil.

Her heart pumped wildly, beating like a drum as she pushed down his jeans and his boxers, thrilling at the sight of his gorgeous cock, ready for business. She wrapped a hand around him and he groaned her name.

Finally, he freed the condom from the wrapper, and she grabbed it. She rolled the condom on him, loving the way his breath hitched as she touched him. He positioned himself at her entrance, sliding the tip of his dick against her heat, and she gasped. She was electric tonight, poised to spark from a single, sizzling touch. At last, the moment she'd longed for had arrived. He pushed into her, and she was ready to sing hallelujah to the skies.

Her memory had been playing tricks on her. He wasn't just the best.

He was extraordinary. He was out of this world. Nothing had ever felt so damn good. This was the very definition of ecstasy. He sank so deep inside her that she tensed and tightened around him, intensifying the sensations. She laced her fingers through his hair, her hands gripping his skull as he stroked.

"Is this working?" he said in between pants.

"Hmm? Yeah. It feels amazing."

"That's not what I mean," he said harshly.

"What do you mean?" Her brain was so foggy she couldn't process anything that didn't involve satisfying the sweet ache between her legs. He thrust harder, stilling himself inside her, letting her feel him fill her up. Oh, did she feel it. She felt stretched in the best of ways.

"Is it getting me out of your system?" he asked as he pumped slowly now.

She shook her head. "No. It only makes me want more of you."

"I want more of you, too. I want so much more," he said, driving into her again, a controlled, measured thrust that made her cry out in pleasure.

She'd expected hard and fast sex, the same way he'd kissed her. But this was different. He held her hips. He took his time. He fucked her, deliberately slow, maddeningly controlled, letting her experience how good it was to be taken by him. Reminding her, whether he intended to or not, that he could give her everything she ever wanted in bed. He was masterful, rolling his hips, then pulling back, leaving her wanting more. It was like a claiming, as if he were taking her in a way that made it starkly clear she belonged to him.

She dug her fingernails into his shoulders, trying to draw him closer, even though they were as close as two people could be. She curled a leg around his ass. She wanted to feel him everywhere. Every inch of her skin, every cell, every neuron craved the pleasure.

"I know you like it wild, Cara. But I bet you like it when I fuck you like I own you," he said, his voice all pure raw need, his words sending a fresh wave of sparks through her body. "Because that's how I'm doing it now."

"Yes," she said, her breathing erratic. "I like it all. I like everything with you. You're driving me crazy."

"Good. Because you drive me insane," he said, and for a second he sounded angry, even mad at himself.

She opened her mouth to ask why, but as he swiveled his hips and rocked into her, bringing her so damn close, she knew now was not the time for questions.

"You want to get me out of your system," he said roughly, as his fingers dug into her hips, leaving marks, she was sure. "But maybe I need you out of mine, too. Sometimes it'll be fast, sometimes it'll be hard, sometimes rough, and sometimes it'll be like this."

"I want it every way with you," she said, but then stopped talking because he buried her in a kiss that scorched her. This man consumed her. He stole every breath from her lungs. He could have anything from her.

This was an undoing. This was him unraveling her stitch

by stitch, unknitting all her control, so she was left only this hot, fevered, hungry thing.

Needing him.

He rocked into her like the steady beat of a drum. The persistent climb up the hill. He worked for her pleasure, he took nothing for granted, and he drove her to the very brink.

"Please, Travis. Harder," she cried out. "Please fuck me 'til I come."

"Nothing less, my sweet, dirty girl. Never anything less."

He changed speed. He shifted into high gear, harder, faster, more dangerous. Her back bowed, and her hands clawed at him. He pounded into her, turning the slow, hot, wet slides into the fast and furious friction that her body sought greedily. She was ravenous for him; her heart spun wildly in her chest and her body sang with rapture.

She cried out his name, like a chant, as she came so hard her vision blurred. She nearly collapsed in his arms from the neon bliss that bathed her brain and washed over every inch of her.

Then her name echoed, too, in the air, a low, hot growl in her ear, the sound of him wanting this connection, this combustible reaction as much as she did. His hands gripped her as he came inside her on a wild grunt.

Chapter Fifteen

Travis groaned happily as he took another forkful of the pasta primavera she'd whipped up, courtesy of Giada from the Food Network. He pointed to the dish and nodded in appreciation. His obvious delight in her cooking pleased her.

"I'm glad you like it."

"This might be the best pasta dish I've ever had that doesn't include meat," he said.

Cara laughed. "Thank you for that caveat on your praise."

He pretended to peer into the serving bowl on the table on her back porch. "Well, I hunted around and found no chicken."

"Now I really can't wait to feed you my famous risotto with snap peas or the fettuccine with figs and goat cheese," she joked.

"Funny. I didn't hear tri-tip steak in those dishes."

"Nor will you."

"You used to eat burgers, though? Didn't you?"

"I did. But I'm not a huge meat eater now." She took another bite of the pasta, followed by a sip of her chardonnay to chase it. Tonight was a great evening. Hot sex against the wall, a good meal under the setting sun and a warm breeze, and her dog lying peacefully in the grass several feet away from the table. Add in the fact that Henry was resting quietly, too, rather than begging for scraps, and she was sure this night might enter the record books as the most perfect evening ever for Cara Bailey.

"Why's that?"

She gestured to the two dogs, who'd become buddies. Henry's back legs were splayed out behind him, giving him a Super Dog look. "I work with animals for a living. I'd rather not rely on them for nutrition, too. Besides, I get everything I need from veggies and noodles and so on."

He eyed her up and down, deliberately appraising her. "So that's where your figure comes from. Body courtesy of carrots and broccoli."

"And don't forget the other benefit—more carrots means I don't feel guilty about eating cookies. I can't wait to dive into the batch you brought. I just hope they're as good as the dog biscuits Henry gave me," she said with a wink.

He held up a beer bottle to toast. "Here's hoping I can keep pace with my dog."

She finished another bite of the veggies then set down her fork. "Seriously though, Travis. I appreciate all of this—the cookies, the flowers, and fixing my car." As she recounted the kind gestures, her heart beat a quick and happy rhythm that seemed to come out of nowhere. She nearly brought her hand to her chest to settle it down, because why on earth would it be all fluttery like that?

He gestured to the food on the table. "And I really appreciate the extra effort you've gone to with Henry, and with this amazing meal," he said, keeping up with the compliments, too. "I've just now decided it's as good as any pasta dish, even with meat."

She rolled her eyes. "Now you're just trying to ply me with praise to get in my pants again," she said, because it was better to keep the focus on the out-of-this-world connection they shared between their bodies, rather than on the easy way they had of talking, of laughing, of leaning on each other. A wisp of worry crawled up her spine, reminding her to be careful, not to linger on those other things.

"Then let's finish dinner, because once with you is never enough for me," he said in a voice both sexy and tender. Her heart dared to soar, and she wanted to smack the damn thing with a fly swatter for reacting simply to his tone. These stupid feelings that had the audacity to surface needed to be quelled immediately.

She peered at the dogs, still lounging in the grass, choosing to focus on them. "Tell me, how did you pick the name Henry? It's not a common name for a dog."

There. Better. Dogs were neutral ground. Travis took a swallow of his beer and leaned back in his chair. "Henry," he said, stroking his chin, his eyes getting a faraway look. "It's kind of a funny story."

"Tell me," she said, clasping her hands under her chin.

"Henry was my firehouse mentor. He worked with my dad. He was basically my father's closest friend in the battalion. Battled many a fire together. He was there the night my dad died," Travis said, taking a deep breath as he spoke.

A lump rose in her throat. She scooted closer, resting a hand on his arm.

"Henry didn't try to be a surrogate father or anything," Travis continued, "which was probably good. Because I'm kind of stubborn, as you may have noticed," he said, stopping to flash a quick smile.

She nodded and smiled, too, then let him continue.

"And I probably wouldn't have taken well to that. But he looked out for me when my dad was gone. I was ten, and he made sure I didn't lose my way after that, you know? I think all the guys knew that Megan and I were kind of these lone kids for a bit, and while I looked after her, Henry could sense that I needed someone when my mom was struggling. So he'd bring me by the firehouse, and he'd check in, and as I grew older, he was the one who taught me the basics of fighting fires."

She squeezed his arm. "I love that you had someone there for you. Who could be that person you needed."

Travis nodded and swallowed hard. Maybe he was holding back painful memories. It had to be painful, losing a parent. He was a tough guy, who didn't show too many emotions, so even the barest sliver revealed tugged at her.

"I did need someone. Henry was definitely that guy. He meant a lot to me. He was the one who taught me how to play cards, too," he said.

Her eyes widened. "He really did have a big impact on you." She took a beat, then asked, "Is he still around?"

"He's retired. Moved to San Diego. I hear from him now and then. He's enjoying the sun and the surf and his woman. He and his wife have been married for forty years."

"Same as my parents," she said.

"What about you? Anything special to Violet's name?" he said, tipping his chin to her black and white border collie. Violet's head tilted to the side, and she raised an ear when she heard herself being discussed.

"You're a good girl," Cara said to her best friend. She turned her attention back to Travis. "I wish I had a great story like that. And truth be told, I once thought about naming her after my birth mom."

"You did?"

"I was twelve when I thought that. That was when I had my"—she stopped to sketch air quotes—"*birth mom phase.*"

"What's a birth mom phase?" he asked with a laugh.

"Oh, it's just that time when I asked more questions and all. My parents were great. They answered everything they could, though their info was pretty limited. My birth mom was from Nevada, she was sixteen when she had me, and that's all I knew. But I had this fantasy that I'd find out her name, and we'd have picnics and go shopping, and I'd name a dog after her at some point, since we always had dogs growing up."

"Did you ever? Find out her name? Don't tell me it was Violet because that would be too wild a coincidence for us to have both done something kind of similar," he said, gesturing from her to him and then to their dogs.

She smiled and shook her head, a bit of a wistful sigh escaping her lips. "I just picked Violet because it's my favorite color and it's a pretty name. And as for the phase, well, like all good phases, I grew out of it."

"Did you ever find your birth mom? Did you want to?"

She shook her head. "No. Even though it was a closed adoption, there are processes in place now and I could probably track her down, but I decided I didn't have to. There's nothing I really *need* to know. I'm just glad the fates aligned when I was born and *my* parents were the ones who got to have me," she said, shooting him a smile.

"Me, too," he said softly, and then took her hand off his arm and threaded his fingers through hers. Squeezing her gently. Tugging her close. If she thought her heart was dancing earlier, that was nothing compared to the way it swayed toward him as he said, "Because that means you wound up in my hometown."

Oh dear lord. Her heart soared off like a kite.

Then he kissed her. It wasn't the heated, crazed kiss in the doorway. It was sweeter, softer, gentler. It was an evening kiss as the sun dropped below the horizon, and it spoke of the two of them, and how they were coming together in more ways than she'd intended.

That was the big problem.

She was getting in over her head. Having a two-week tryst with Travis Jansen might not have been her brightest idea. As the night rolled on, and he helped clean the dishes, and kissed the back of her neck, and handed her a chocolate chip cookie that he'd baked for her, she knew her heart was far too involved. When the clock ran out in another week, she was sure to leave this fling with a big old wound in that organ in her chest.

Because it was so much more than a fling.

• • •

Maybe there was something in the water. He'd need to get a water testing kit. Conduct an inspection. See if there were chemicals that were making his brain play tricks on him.

Because as Travis drove home, he could distinctly recall having instructed his brain to focus solely on the sex. And the sex had been spectacular, so he'd really like some answers as to where the hell his damn heart had hid his calm, cool, rational mind for the evening. He'd like to know why the hell he'd shared that stuff with her about Henry. He had some questions for himself, too, as to why he'd acted all domestic, not to mention intimate in a way that went well beyond the physical, and why on earth he'd let those words about how glad he was that she lived here tumble free.

But the reality was this—he was glad she was here. She made him happy.

That was the big problem.

He had no idea what to do with a woman who made him feel…*something*.

Not a single fucking clue.

He turned into his driveway and slammed his car into park. He dropped his forehead to the steering wheel and blew out a long, frustrated sigh.

Something wet was on his face. Something slobbery and long. Travis looked up to find Henry licking his cheek. He laughed and pulled the little guy in for a quick hug.

"Let's take you for a walk. Clear our heads," Travis said, and the two of them hopped out of the car. Henry was already leashed up, so they headed down his street, their path illuminated by streetlamps that glowed faintly, casting sickles of pale yellow light on the sidewalk. Every crunch of his boots on the sidewalk echoed; every click of Henry's nails sounded. They were man and dog alone in the inky black night, blanketed by the quiet of their small town—the very town he'd said he was so damn glad Cara had arrived in many years ago. He shook his head. What had gotten into him?

Henry stopped to sniff some flowers edging a neighbor's lawn, and Travis quickly tugged his leash so the dog wouldn't be tempted to water them. Instead, Henry found a fire hydrant around the corner where he left his mark.

They walked on through the night, block after block, quiet sleepy section of town through quiet sleepy section of town, until they'd wandered smack-dab into the town square. Travis scratched his head and uttered a *huh*.

He hadn't planned on coming here, but somehow this was where his feet had taken him—to his friend who'd been a lot like him. The Panting Dog was closed for the night, but when Travis peered inside, he spotted Becker behind the bar, cleaning up. Megan must be feeling better, and that thought brought a smile to his face. Henry parked himself in a sit and whimpered loudly. Travis imagined the dog was asking, *What are we doing?*

"That's a good question, buddy. What are we doing?"

Travis didn't have any answers, so he rapped on the glass.

Becker looked up, nodded, and came out from behind the bar to unlock the door.

"How's Megan?"

"She's better. Sound asleep now, so I came back to finish up some work. You need a beer? Cause you look like you need a beer."

A smile flickered briefly on his face. "Is it that obvious?"

Becker clapped him on the back. "It's nearly one in the morning, and you don't live that close to my bar. It *is* that obvious. Just don't tell the health inspector I let a dog in,"

Becker said as he locked the door behind them.

"Henry keeps all my secrets," Travis said as he pulled up a stool and sat down, the dog sitting at his feet.

Becker poured a beer from the tap and slid it across the counter. Travis knocked back a long swallow, savoring the taste. The two men didn't say much, but there wasn't much to say. Travis was living in a foreign land, with his two feet in the middle of a swamp of uncertainty.

"So," Becker began, taking his time with his words, it seemed. "How was your night with Cara?"

There was no ribbing in his tone this time. The man wasn't giving him a hard time like he'd done at his house earlier that evening. This question was as straightforward as they came.

"It was good," Travis answered, because that was the full truth. His time with Cara was incredibly good.

"And is it good or bad that your night was so good?" Becker asked, as he wiped a rag across the counter.

Travis took another drink, enjoying the fizz of the pale ale. "That, my friend, is the question."

His buddy shot him a small smile. "I take it the answer is hard to come by?"

"It is."

Becker tucked the rag under the sink then rested his palms on the counter. "You'll figure it out soon enough, and when you do, I trust it'll be worth it."

Worth it.

But what was so worthwhile about feeling this way? About operating without any compass to rely on? He wasn't so sure if he even wanted to dig more to find out. The kind of excavation required was too daunting.

He set down the glass, trying to center himself, to find some roots back to the things he knew—the cards, the firehouse, his friendships.

"Want to play a round of poker?" he asked. Because cards always made sense, even when everything else blinked in and out of focus.

Becker shook his head. "Can't. After I close up, I need to get home to Megan. Another time."

Another time.

The way things were changing around him, "other times" were becoming fewer and farther between.

Chapter Sixteen

The next few days rolled by in a hot summer haze of sex, food, and dog lessons. It was bliss for Cara, especially as she tried her best to ignore the inevitable expiration date that loomed.

For starters, just three nights after their dinner date, Henry demonstrated his quick learning by sitting on each corner before crossing the street during the training walk.

Then they returned to her house, where she fed Travis her risotto with snap peas. The addition of dinner to their fling happened naturally, like a new unwritten item on the daily agenda, and one that suited them both. A working man, with a working man's appetite, Travis liked to eat. Cooking was one of Cara's true passions, and having someone to share a dish with made it all the better.

"What are you doing to me, woman?" he said as he finished the first serving and ladled a second one onto his plate. "Your cooking is too good."

She beamed, and after the dishes were washed and put away, he showed her other uses for her kitchen counter. Amazing how that surface provided the perfect angle and height for multiple orgasms. Or maybe it was just that Travis had made it his specialty to deliver them to her.

By the next Monday, Henry had started to come when called, an important milestone for a dog's training. To celebrate, Cara whipped up fettuccine with figs and goat cheese.

"You've put a voodoo hex on me by making me like food that doesn't have meat," Travis declared, as he finished a fig while they ate dinner on the deck.

"You've figured me out."

"Did you learn all this from the Food Network?" he asked, gesturing to the dishes on the table.

She nodded. "Amazing what TV can teach you."

He narrowed his eyes at her. "And you sure you weren't just watching for Bobby Flay? Admit it, you had a crush on him," he said, staring at her intensely, as if she'd reveal a secret.

She laughed and shook her head. "I swear I only watch for the food. As a matter of fact, I learned how to make the best eggplant Parmesan in the world from Mr. Flay. Maybe if you're good, I'll make that after the next lesson."

He placed his hands together as if praying. "I'm a lucky man. My dog is learning how to steal the show when he goes on stage, and you're feeding me the best meals ever. Are you sure there isn't anything I can do for you? Well, besides make you come more times than you can count," he said with a wink as he polished off his dinner.

She leaned forward in her chair, letting her long hair brush against his arm, knowing that undid him. He groaned, low and raspy, giving away his quick rise on the scale of desire. "That seems pretty reasonable," she said in her best sultry voice. "But since you asked, my dryer has been rattling loudly on the high efficiency cycle. Can you fix it?"

Twenty minutes later, the dryer was remarkably silent as it tumbled through clothes, and Cara was loud as can be as he showed her how highly efficient he was at cycling through all the non-bed surfaces in her house.

After he left that night, she locked the door and hummed a Jane Black tune as she wandered into the kitchen to turn on the dishwasher. For the briefest of moments, she imagined he was still here, brushing his teeth in the master bathroom, sliding under the sheets, waiting for her. She pictured returning to him, night after night, doing all these domestic things together, and then all the dirty things after dark, too.

Everything.

The images were so intoxicating to her commitment-craving heart that they started to feel real, like she could have this kind of life with him.

"Don't be foolish," she muttered.

She squeezed her eyes shut, as if she were waking herself from a dream. That fantasy life with him could never happen with him. She had to practice some self-control.

She stabbed the start button on the dishwasher, shaking her head in disgust at her runaway thoughts. Here she was, playing house with him, feeding him, treating him like he was on the path to becoming the man of her future. But he was merely the man of the present, and she needed to keep him in that box. This kind of affair was a tropical vacation. It was waterfalls and lagoons, hammocks and aquamarine waters. Blissful, intoxicating, and also completely illusory. It was ticking ever closer to the end, and in a week she'd reenter reality.

She picked up her phone from the kitchen table and scrolled through messages from clients, answering a few before bed. She spotted a note from Joe. The nice guy. The one who actually wanted a future.

Looking forward to seeing you soon. Still up for 'Dinner, Take Two'? No more bad jokes from me. I've got all new material.

She laughed lightly. He had a decent sense of humor. He was kind. She wrote back to confirm their next date. "Looking forward to seeing you next Tuesday! Can't wait to hear the new material. I bet it's fab!"

As she added the date to her calendar, she noted that dinner with Joe fell two days after the fireman's auction.

Perfect timing. The scheduled date kept her on the straight and narrow, blinders on, her focus solely on what it should always have been with Travis—living life for the present, so she could move forward into a new future with someone else.

For a few more days, she had the lease on Travis Jansen, and she intended to use it to the fullest. Soon, so very soon, he'd be gone from her head and her heart.

He had to be.

• • •

The days flew by so fast that Travis wished he could stop time.

He hated for this to end, because a fling with Cara was the greatest thing ever known to man.

Hell, he'd like to exist forever in this bubble of mind-blowing sex, eye-rollingly delicious food, and fantastically-good time spent with the prettiest, sharpest, sweetest woman in the world.

That woman had also worked wonders with his dog. In a short time, Henry had transformed into a model canine citizen, and Travis had become addicted to Cara's cooking.

Okay, fine. He was addicted to her body, too, and to making her come over and over. He couldn't stop touching her and taking her to new heights. Even though their sell-by date loomed ever closer on the calendar, he had more in mind for the woman he was unable to resist.

They finished the day's training session with Henry, practicing his "special trick" for the auction in Travis's driveway. Henry nailed it, and Cara cheered.

"So do I get the eggplant Parmesan now, since Henry has mastered all his obedience lessons?" he asked, as they walked across his lawn.

She smiled faintly but shook her head. "I'd rather skip the meal and go straight to the main attraction. Meaning, let's just have dessert."

He groaned appreciatively. She was the tastiest dessert he'd ever had, so tonight's menu was fine by him. He wanted her food, but he wanted her more, especially when she pressed her body to his the second they reached his front porch. Her hands dipped into the back of his jeans as he fumbled at the lock, then darted around to the front of his briefs as soon as the door opened.

"Damn, you're a feisty one right now," he said as he unclipped Henry and dropped the leash by the door. The dog trotted up the steps to his water bowl on the kitchen floor.

"I am, and I want you now," she said, her eyes glittering with desire.

"Fuck dinner. Fuck food. I want you more than all the eggplant in the universe," he said roughly as he lowered his mouth to her lips, kissing her hard, and with the kind of pressure that he knew drove her wild. In mere seconds, she was writhing against him in the entryway, wrapping a leg around his thigh. He tugged her closer, kissing her deeply as she moaned and moved with him. He lowered his hands to her ass, so round and curvy that he simply had to smack it.

She yelped playfully.

That was a very good sign. "Evidently, I haven't spanked you enough. Allow me to rectify that."

"Oh please do. I insist."

"Your insistence will be rewarded," he said, as he smacked her rear. Her eyes lit up like a neon sign blinking *more*. "You do have the most smackable ass I've ever seen. But let's just slide these off so I can test it for sure," he said, unzipping her jean shorts. She quickly pushed them down to the floor, leaving them in a denim puddle, and he swatted her once more.

She cried out in pleasure, a gorgeous, sexy moan escaping her ruby red lips. From the living room, it sounded as if Henry had joined in with a bark of his own.

He ignored the dog, because the sight of Cara in front of him, half-naked, and ready for more of his open palm was enticing. Besides, the entryway seemed as good a place as any for a quick round of spanking and fucking, and fucking and spanking. He ran a finger against her mouth, his appetite for her multiplying as she parted her lips and sighed sexily. A flush darkened the bare skin above her tank top.

He craved turning her on, like nothing he'd experienced. He longed to explore every avenue of sex with her, to know her body in every way, even this way—with the slightest bit of pain and pleasure mingled together. But as he dropped his hand once more to swat her rear, Henry voiced his opinion again.

And he had one hell of an opinion.

The Jack Russell barked loudly. It was a demanding sound. A *what the hell gives?* noise. Travis broke contact to check on him. Henry sat at the top of the stairs, barking with his snout high in the air, the expression on his face one of complete dissatisfaction with the people.

"What the...?"

Then it hit Travis. He had a hunch that Henry wasn't so fond of what Travis was doing with his palm. Testing the canine, Travis lifted his hand in the air, as if he were about to spank Cara.

The bark turned into a furious howl.

Travis widened his eyes and turned to Cara. She'd clasped her palm over her mouth in surprise.

"Apparently he disapproves of spanking," he said with a wry smile.

"Quite a bit."

Travis tipped his head to the dog and joked. "Think you can train that out of him?"

"I can honestly say I'd never had to train a dog to stop barking when a person is being spanked in the heat of the moment," she said, her lips curved in a naughty grin. "But I know I can figure it out. Just, maybe, not this second. Because I'd rather—"

"Be spanked again?"

"Something like that," she said suggestively.

"Let me put him in the yard, and I can spank you on my bed."

She froze when he said that word. *Bed.* They hadn't made it to the bed during this fling; that had been intentional. He wasn't quite sure why he'd suggested it now, or if there was something *more* to his unexpected change of tune. But before he could try to make sense of it himself, she shook her head, and said, "Let's trade places with Henry. Leave him in the house. We'll go outside."

He wasn't about to argue with having Cara al fresco, so he grabbed a towel from the linen closet and headed outside, shutting the door behind him, leaving Henry to stare forlornly at the sliding glass.

His fence was high and neighbors shouldn't be able to see, but even if they did, he honestly didn't care. Not when Cara tugged off her tank top, unsnapped her bra, and stepped out of her panties in less than ten seconds.

She worked his zipper down as he grabbed a condom from his pocket. Soon, they were both in full birthday suits, the warm air on their skin. She dropped to her hands and knees, presenting her creamy skin for another swatting. He happily obliged, once, twice, three times, savoring her heated reaction to each smack. He didn't hit her hard; he used just the right amount of pressure to make her moan and wriggle. Then he smoothed his hand over her backside, rubbing out the sting. His fingers darted between her legs.

Oh fuck. She was liquid. Need slammed into him when he felt her wetness. "You're so turned on right now, aren't you?" The question was a rhetorical one, because the evidence was incontrovertible.

"Everything you do turns me on, Travis," she said, looking back at him, the expression in her eyes both lustful and trusting. God, she was stunning, so confident and so honest with her own sexuality. It floored him and stoked his desire at the same time.

"You've been bad enough. I have to be inside you now," he said, then wasted no time rolling on the condom. He gripped her hips and sank into her.

A tremor of intense pleasure rolled through him as he filled her completely.

They both moaned in unison.

Then he took her.

He held on tight, driving into her furiously, sinking as deep into her as he could go. The sound of their bodies slapping together urged him on. His blood roared, his heart pounded, her moans triggering a fresh round of pleasure in his body.

There was nothing else in the world but this animalistic fever as he thrust faster, harder, deeper. He reached for her hair, twisting it in his fist and gripping hard. He slinked his other hand around her waist, dropping it between her legs as he thrust. He rubbed her clit, coaxing an orgasm from her as she cried out, "I'm coming."

Then, he pulled her up, so he was sitting on his knees and they were both upright as he thrust into her like that. Her body aligned beautifully with his. He swore he'd never experienced anything like this connection before. The intensity blew his mind. It torched his body. In his arms, she was his completely, and that's where he wanted her, chasing the edge of bliss with him and him alone.

"We fucking fit perfectly, don't we?" he said roughly in her ear as his spine ignited with the start of his own climax.

"So perfectly," she echoed as she rocked back and he drove into her, coming with her in a cacophony of moans and groans and cries.

Soon, he eased out, looped his arms around her, and tugged her in close, pulling her next to him on the towel. She sighed, a lovely, contented sound that warmed his heart.

He blinked.

That was strange. It was utterly weird to switch from that kind of furious fucking, to this kind of cuddling. Funny, how he could go from claiming her like a wild man—they were goddamn animals screwing doggy style, for fuck's sake—to wanting to hold her close. It was the oddest changeup he'd ever felt, having these two conflicting wishes present in his heart at once.

But, he thought, as his rational, risk-assessing mind kicked back in, as long as he kept those wishes separate, he'd be safe.

Besides, they'd both be in the clear in a few days, when moments like these ended. They'd move on—him to his single ways, her to...

The thought of her moving on was a kick in his chest. It was far too unpleasant for him to consider when she was here in his arms, all soft and snug.

Henry pawed at the sliding glass door, whining. Travis found himself wishing that Cara could start the *I'm-cool-with-you-spanking-her* training stat, so that he could do this again, and again, and again.

He chuckled silently. He could barely believe he wanted a dog who was trained not to cock block a spanking.

But what he really wanted was for this not to end.

Chapter Seventeen

The trap had been set.

All that was left in these two weeks of training was for Henry to prove he'd mastered his instincts and could find the will to resist something succulent.

Cara waited patiently on the park bench. She wore a short little skirt and a red shirt, and those legs he adored were on display in the June sun. He looked in her direction and she waved. He nodded back.

Cara's sister Stacy was strolling nonchalantly around the town square, having volunteered to be the guinea pig to tempt his dog.

Stacy was perfect for the job because Henry hadn't met her yet. She was as much a stranger as anyone would ever be, and behaving himself in front of a person he'd never met would be a huge accomplishment and a big sign that he was ready for the fireman's auction—ready to save the day for the Families of Fallen Firefighters.

Henry walked in a perfect heel, ignoring all the other dogs out for late afternoon walks. He stayed in a trot, keeping pace with Travis, exactly what he'd have to do on stage that coming weekend.

A brief fleet of nerves docked in Travis's chest as Henry neared Stacy. This would be a hard task for any dog. Especially a lover of treats and an aficionado of ladies' legs, because he was about to be tempted by both. Travis hoped fiercely that Henry would prove his mettle as the very pregnant Stacy approached him.

Stacy pointed at Henry and called out loudly, "Oh my god, your dog is so cute. What's his name?"

Travis answered as he stopped walking. "This is Henry. He's a Jack Russell."

"Can I pet him?"

"Of course."

Carefully, with a hand on her big belly, Stacy bent down and scratched Henry's chin. The dog's ears perked up, and then his snout rose in the air. Travis tensed. "C'mon buddy. You can do it," he said under his breath, because it was obvious Henry had sniffed the most delicious thing in the world.

The peanut butter slathered on Stacy's leg.

One hundred percent pure dog trap.

Travis imagined Henry was floating on a cloud of dog lust right now, fantasizing about licking every last bit off Cara's sister's leg. He sniffed again and tried briefly to inch closer and lap up the goods, but Travis uttered a firm command. "Sit, Henry."

And the dog obeyed, his rear going straight to the ground. From several feet away, Cara clapped in glee. Travis glanced over at her; she was beaming. She had known exactly how to handle both dog and owner, and help them realize their full potential. Travis had no guarantee of winning anything, but he was confident that his secret weapon was locked and loaded, even though it meant the end of the most fantastic two-week tryst of his life.

• • •

As she walked over to the three of them, Cara held her shoulders high, a burst of pride in her chest at the little dog's progress.

"He did great," she said, bending down to scratch Henry's chin in praise. Then she rose, doing her best to put on a happy face. She *was* genuinely happy, but she was also sad that Henry's success meant Travis no longer needed her. Their days were numbered in the low single digits now. "Both of you did. You're going to be fantastic this weekend," she said, as brightly as she could.

Travis draped an arm around her briefly, and the move felt like it was just for her, even though his words were for all ears. "We're lucky to have a very good teacher."

Stacy pointed to the dog. "I'm very impressed with him. He sure seems ready. But you?" She arched an eyebrow and appraised Travis's appearance from head to toe. Cara furrowed her brow because she couldn't figure out what issue Stacy could possibly have with this handsome specimen of man—he was the fantasy fireman, from his firm, sturdy arms, to his broad, strapping chest, to that gorgeous face and piercing blue eyes, and the thick, dark hair that Cara loved running her fingers through. Come to think of it, that hair was the ideal length for holding onto, as Cara had noticed the last few times she'd been with him.

"Me?" Travis asked, tilting his head to the side.

Stacy reached out and fingered a strand of his hair. "You might want to consider stopping by for a little trim. Ladies do like a nice, crisp cut on a man. It might make you even more handsome."

A plume of jealousy flared up in Cara's chest. *Ladies.* Anyone out there—in Hidden Oaks, in the county, in the whole damn state—could win Travis. Even if it was only for one date, the notion of him out with anyone but her was a black cloud darkening her day.

He turned to Cara. "What do you think? Do I need a trim?" His voice was soft and low, and it seemed to feather over her skin and skim down her back. Warmth shimmied along her spine from the way his gaze locked with hers.

A few strands of his hair fell onto his forehead. Before she thought better off it, she brushed them away from his eyes. He seemed to be holding his breath, or maybe he was holding back, fighting the overwhelming urge to touch her, too. Maybe he was even remembering last night, when they'd christened her washing machine since they'd already broken in the dryer, and he'd rocked her world to the spin cycle. Or her couch the night before, when she'd straddled him and rode him hard, reverse cowgirl style. Hell, she was thinking of all those times, because the last several days had passed in a blur of wild sex and intensive dog training.

She'd forced herself to focus on those two things only, working hard to avoid pesky matters like feelings. During their brief affair, Cara had kept her schedule as packed as a can of sardines, as if bookending Travis would insulate her from wanting more than she already had from that man. She reasoned that if their evenings always had an end in sight, the re-entry into the Travis-less, post-fling world in a few days wouldn't be a cruel awakening.

That's what she'd told herself, every time he'd said something sweet, did something kind, made her laugh.

He'd outlined his position on relationships quite clearly, so there was no reason to think the two of them would ever amount to more than these few weeks. So she'd applied her best rinse-and-repeat mantra of *just a fling*, reminding herself over and over not to fall head over heels for a man who had made it clear that commitment was a four-letter word.

Hair, however, was a sexy word. She didn't let go of his hair, just kept running it between her thumb and forefinger, as if no one else was around, considering if he needed a trim. "I think you'd look quite handsome with a haircut," she said softly, and it was as if they existed in a cocoon of togetherness there in the town square, even though his dog and her sister were next to them.

Stacy cleared her throat. "Well, I think I'd better head back to work and get this peanut butter off my legs. Feel free to stop by for a cut. I'll be open for another hour," she said, then turned toward the salon.

"Should I take her up on her offer now?"

Cara dropped her hand on his arm, stopping him. "No. I have a better idea."

• • •

The bell tinkled on the door to Stacy's salon as Cara slipped inside, a latte in hand. She'd popped into the local coffee shop before stopping by. Stacy was applying color to the

Hidden Oaks librarian's hair, a young and pretty blonde named Kelly. Cara knew her because she'd taken Stacy's four-year-old son to the library occasionally for story time.

"Hi, Cara," Kelly said as she headed to the booth. "Is Travis all ready for the Bachelor Fireman's Auction this weekend?"

Cara stopped in her tracks and shot her sister a curious look.

"What? Was it some secret that you're prepping him?" Stacy said, giving Cara a *What gives?* shrug.

"No. Of course not," she said, not entirely surely why she'd frozen at the mention of his name. Maybe it was because she and Travis were linked together, but not quite linked the way she wanted.

"Hey, Kelly. You should bid on Travis," Stacy said, nudging Kelly's shoulder.

The flicker of jealousy came roaring back, headstrong and fierce. Cara swore she would breathe fire if she spoke. She clamped her lips shut.

Kelly laughed politely and shook her head. "Oh, I don't know that I would ever have the guts to do that," she said.

"You so can," Stacy said, egging her on. "You've got the funds, don't you? Didn't you sell a matchmaking app to some tech giant? Opening bids for the men are usually around five hundred dollars and the money goes to charity."

"That is true. I do have enough," Kelly said, biting her lip as if she were noodling on the idea of bidding on Cara's man. Cara had half a mind to tackle her sister. The presence of that huge basketball in Stacy's mid-section kept her wedge sandals firmly rooted to the hardwood floor. "Maybe I could. The money does go to a good cause, and he's single and all."

Cara clenched her fists, her right hand nearly crushing the coffee cup. Stacy wrapped a piece of tinfoil around a strand of Kelly's hair, continuing her push. "Besides, if it's not you, it'll be some grand old dame of the vineyards who makes a play for him. You *have* to go for it, don't you think, Cara?"

Cara narrowed her eyes, positive that red clouds were billowing out of them. "Sure," she muttered, then finished off her drink and tossed the cup in the paper-recycling bin.

Stacy patted Kelly's shoulder. "Let's get you under the hairdryer, hon."

After Stacy settled Kelly under the heat, Cara grabbed her sister's arm and pulled her to the front of the salon. "What was that all about?" she asked through gritted teeth.

"What do you mean?" Stacy asked, batting her eyes.

She pointed. "You know what I mean. Why would you tell Kelly to bid on Travis?"

"You trained him and his dog. You want him to do well, don't you?"

"Y-Yes," she said, sputtering. "But…"

"But what?" Stacy parked her hands on her hips, arching an eyebrow in some sort of dare.

Cara heaved a deep sigh. "But I don't want her bidding on him," she managed to admit.

"Correction. You don't want *anyone* bidding on him," Stacy said, her eyes twinkling with mischief as she punched Cara's arm. "I knew it. And that's exactly why I said that to Kelly. Because you're falling for him."

Cara held her chin up high and crossed her arms as she backpedaled. "I don't know what you're talking about."

Stacy laughed loudly. Pointedly. "Oh, that's a good one.

That's a very good one. Because it was obvious thirty minutes ago, with the way you two were touching each other in the town square, that this little one-and-done plan has become something more. So maybe it's time you did something about it, otherwise somebody else might get him this weekend."

Cara scoffed. "It's just an auction to raise money. No one expects the dates that women bid on will turn into real relationships."

At least she hoped not.

Stacy reached out her hand and rested it on Cara's arm. "You never know how a love might start. For someone, it might start at a fireman's auction. It might begin as fun and games and a bid. But what if someone bids on him and he falls for her because he thinks all you want is sex? There's something between the two of you, and if you don't want other women bidding on him, maybe you should ask yourself if you'd truly be happy just letting this be a fling."

Cara swallowed. Her mouth was dry. Her brain was fuzzy. She hated that Stacy was seeing right through her defenses. But she was also glad that she could finally stop keeping these feelings tied up in her chest. She *had* to free them. "I know," she admitted softly, looking down at her sandaled feet. "But I know it's going to end, so I'm just trying to enjoy it while I can."

Stacy lifted Cara's chin gently. "Maybe it doesn't have to end. Maybe it can be the beginning. Try letting him know how you feel."

"*I* don't even know how I feel," she said quietly, her voice threatening to break. Her heart was playing a vicious tug of war with her head, yanking hard on all of her future plans, trying to knock them on their ass with this one crazy desire—her deep longing for Travis. She simply didn't want her time with him to end. She wanted to keep going, with no end in sight. But the trouble was what it always had been—he didn't want the things that were so important to her, the things that spelled happiness. She'd seen the road-map. She'd studied it as a bystander as Stacy and Sofie had traveled down the path. The husband, the kids, the white picket fence—she longed for the life her two sisters had. She yearned not to be the odd woman out. She was already something of a curiosity in her family, given her unconventional arrival in the clan. She didn't want to remain that way, and she didn't know how to settle for less than all this happiness she saw around her—in her parents, in her sisters, in her friends.

"Yes, you do. Now what can I do for you? I need to tend to Kelly."

"Can I borrow a pair of scissors?"

"Good thing I taught you the basics of a good cut long ago." Stacy raised an eyebrow approvingly. "I trust Travis won't be needing my services."

Cara shook her head. She was going to take care of him all by herself.

Chapter Eighteen

Cara was quiet as she wet Travis's hair with a spray bottle. She didn't say much, either, as she sat him down in a wooden chair on her deck, under the setting sun. Trying to give voice to the jumbled mess of emotions that darted and dodged and played havoc in her heart was too hard.

She focused on the task at hand. She didn't want anyone else making him look as handsome as he could possibly be. She was the woman who would make him the top pick. Draping a towel over his shoulders, she began her work. She knew how to manage a basic cut, thanks to her sister.

"How short are you going to go?" he asked. Henry was back at Travis's house, and Violet was resting on her dog bed inside.

"Marine short. That work for you?"

He craned his neck to look up at her. "Do whatever you think will look good."

Her heart fluttered ever so briefly from the way his eyes

stayed fixed on her for a beat.

"I'm not really going to cut it that short. Just a trim will do," she said. She planted her feet apart and ran her fingers through his hair. His breath hitched as she touched him. His shoulders tightened, and for some reason his reaction sent goose bumps racing across her skin.

He whispered her name. That was all he said. Nothing more, but it was the low, sexy tone that conveyed some kind of untapped need that made her heart beat wildly.

"I'm glad you're letting me do this," she said.

"Me, too. I much prefer your hands on me."

She reached for the comb she'd placed on the table and grasped a few strands, combing neatly through, and then holding the hair between her fingers. With the scissors in her other hand, she snipped the ends. "I didn't think it was too long. But I do think this will look nice," she said, and her voice felt like it was coming from somewhere else, from some woman who was making idle chitchat because she didn't know how to say the other things. The harder things. She wasn't entirely sure how to voice all that she felt because she wasn't even sure what she was feeling, or if this feeling even had a name she could breathe out loud.

She zeroed in on his dark strands, methodically working her way across his head, snipping and cutting, letting the short ends fall to the wooden slats of her deck. He closed his eyes, his lips parted. He looked peaceful and relaxed, like a man enjoying his woman's touch at the end of the day. For a brief moment she could see days like this unspooling before them—cutting his hair, rubbing his shoulders, making him dinner. All while he fixed the pipe under the sink, kissed the back of her neck, asked how her day was.

Damn, that was a potent vision, and she tried desperately to shake it off, as she'd managed to do the last time it had visited her. Because she couldn't ask for *that*, could she? That wasn't what Stacy had wanted her to do, was it? She zeroed in on simpler matters. She snipped and trimmed the top of his head down to his neck, keeping the sections tight and even. She reached the back of his hair, cleaning up the soft little fuzz on his neck.

"You look good," she said softly.

"Thank you. I think this is my favorite haircut ever."

She laughed. "I'm sure."

"No, it is. You have the magic touch."

She cupped his shoulders, so tempted to lean in and plant a kiss on his neck, on the top of his head. He reached up and clasped her hand briefly, unleashing a ribbon of heat in her. She finished the back of his head and walked around to face him.

"How do I look?" he asked, wiggling his eyebrows.

"Hot," she said with a broad smile. This was easy. She could do this part. The last few weeks had shown her how easily they could be playful and dirty with each other. Saying anything more was riskier.

She leaned forward. "Let me just fix up the front of your hair."

She inched closer, wedging her leg between his.

"Make sure this part takes a nice long time," he whispered, his voice dropping low and husky. "I'm enjoying the view."

She glanced down to realize her breasts were eye level with him. She scooted even closer, and he groaned. "Yeah, definitely the best haircut any man anywhere has ever gotten," he added.

The heat inside her turned into a fire as he raised his hands to grip her hips. "Travis," she chided.

"What? You can't cut my hair with my hands on you?"

"I can," she said, because she was almost done. He started rubbing his thumbs against her hips. "But I don't want to slip."

He stilled his hands as she finished snipping. She stretched across him to set the scissors down on the table.

"You might want to take a shower to get all the hair off your neck."

"Only if you shower with me. Or come and find me in the shower," he added, reminding her of her fantasy.

"That does sound nice. But do you want me to get you a mirror, so you can see how it looks?"

He shook his head, and in a blur he pulled her down on top of him in the chair, cupped her cheeks in his hands. "I don't want to see. I don't care. I just want you," he said, and then he kissed her neck, blazing a hot trail along her throat, marking her with his lips.

"So take me. Here and now," she said, because those were the easiest words to say to him. They were wholly true. The other words she had to say were too big, too much to just let slip out unprepared. She needed time to shape them and mold them. And right now, her brain was taking a backseat to her body, so she let her body rule the rest of the day.

She rocked back and forth on him, rubbing against his hard-on through their clothes. Her skirt rode up to her hips. He groaned, and that sexy, needy sound thrilled her. She pressed harder against him, riding the firm ridge through their layers as she straddled him in the deck chair. There was just something so deliciously dirty about a good dry fuck. It was the prelude, the frenzied, fevered build to more. This was a sign of the kind of intensity that two people could have together. To rub, and bump and grind like this—to *want* to—was some kind of late-night fantasy come true.

She picked up the pace, rocking faster, harder, seeking more friction.

She panted.

He groaned.

A bead of sweat rolled down her neck. Even that seemed fitting for this moment, for this kind of joyride of a summer fling. They were summer. They were the setting sun, blazing against the sky, flaring brightly before burning out. This might be one of their last times, and she intended to enjoy every second of the contact with him.

He smothered her with kisses along the bare skin of her neck, her chest, her shoulders, as she thrust against him, his hard length meeting her heat. The friction between them ignited all the atoms and cells inside her, sending sparks of pleasure on a wild roller coaster spin throughout her body. She gripped his shoulders, riding him like a cowgirl atop her horse.

Closing her eyes, she parted her lips and moaned so loudly she would ordinarily have been embarrassed that such an animalistic noise had come from her. Except, there was no room for embarrassment. She was living in a land of pleasure, and there was only room there for wild abandon.

The crest of an orgasm came into view. *"Travis."* His name was a primal cry. "I can't believe I'm doing this."

"Why?" He gripped her hips; his hold on her was relentless, as if he never intended to let go.

"Because I'm dry humping you. I haven't done this in years," she breathed out on a heavy pant, rocking against him.

"Don't stop 'til you come. You hear me?" His voice was an order.

"Yes."

"Promise me you'll keep riding me like this." Now, a firm command.

"I will."

He ran his finger over her lips. "Say it," he said, so in charge of her pleasure, even like this. "Say you won't stop 'til you're shouting my name."

That was all she needed to know. That he was loving this as much as she was. That he wanted to see her get off as badly as she wanted to come. She barely knew who she was with him. One touch, one look, and he had sent her from zero to teetering close in seconds. That's where she was right now. Skating that fine, ecstatic edge of bliss.

Rubbing against his dick.

Grinding her crotch into his.

"I won't stop. I promise. I won't stop 'til I come," she said, squeezing her eyes shut as white-hot bursts streaked through her.

It was like being back in time, when having clothes on didn't prevent you from getting off, when sometimes the first time you come with someone was when you're both fully dressed. Maybe that was what felt so deliciously sinful about how close she was to the finish line. Because this was elementary, this was two plus two, this was the ABCs of chemistry. She rocked crazily against his cock, the hard length of him serving as the launching pad, the hungry kisses on her neck the fuel, his hands traveling all over her body the final turn of the ignition. Then his lips dropped onto hers, and he claimed her mouth, kissing her greedily and sending her flying to the other side. Somehow it felt as if his kisses alone were making her come. She cried out in his mouth, moaning and groaning as she rode him under the sun, coming hard like she always had with him.

. . .

He barely gave her a second to come down from her high. His need for her was too intense, too strong. His bones were vibrating with this overwhelming urge to take her. Watching her writhe and rock on him, like a fire he couldn't hold on to, was almost too much. His entire body was a cyclone, twisting and curling.

He grasped her hips, stood her up, and tugged off her skirt with superhuman speed. She stepped out of it, and her panties, kicking off her shoes, too. Red-hot desire slammed into him as he looked up at her, savoring the glossy sheen in her beautiful blue eyes, the way they seemed to twinkle in the afterglow of that kind of climax.

"I hope you forgive me for not giving you any time to recover, but I need you now," he told her.

"I hope you forgive me for being greedy and wanting another one," she said, her arms crossing over each other in an X as she grabbed the waistband of her red shirt and yanked it over her head. His breath fled his chest at the sight of her nearly naked, wearing only a red lace bra. He'd seen her in the nude so many times in the last few weeks, not to mention countless times in the past, but every moment took his breath away. He stopped to rake his eyes over her, to memorize the curve of her hips, the strength of her legs, her soft, flat belly. As much as the lust ran rampant in his body, he wanted to enjoy these last few times with her. The fireman's auction ticked closer, and there had been no extension on the lease they'd taken out on each other, so all that was left was milking every last ounce of intensity, of pleasure, of coming together.

"As it turns out, today I am offering a special. Two orgasms for the price of one," he joked as he rose from the chair to unhook her bra. He slid the straps off her shoulders and down her arms, then simply stared at her beautiful bare breasts released from their enclosure, and her nipples, rosy and inviting his lips. Without looking away, he tossed the bra onto the table and murmured *beautiful* as he treated each enticing peak to a kiss.

"I didn't know there was a fee attached," she said breathily, as her hands darted out to unzip his jeans. He managed to drag his lips away from her breasts to yank off his own shirt and take off his jeans.

"Never. I just wanted you to know what a good deal I am," he said with a wink, adding his briefs to the pile of clothes.

"I am well aware of the volume of orgasms you can deliver," she said, as her eyes strayed to his dick. He couldn't deny that he loved that she checked him out.

"Then place your hands on the door, woman, because you're about to get a special deal," he said, and she did as instructed as he snagged a condom from his wallet. Pressing her hands to the glass, she bent her body into an L. She was a vision, all right. Pure, sensual femininity. God, he loved how she had no inhibitions with him. He savored the intensity of her sex drive, how it matched his, how wild and willing she was no matter where they were.

He was so ready to slide into that hot, lush body. He pressed his hands against the soft globes of her ass, his thumbs digging into her flesh. His cock throbbed, aching with the need to fill her, but the sight of her bare glistening pussy was too hard for him to resist.

Change of plans.

"I'm taking a short detour first to my favorite place," he murmured, dropping to his knees.

He raised her ass higher, dipped his mouth to her cheeks, and kissed that sweet, sexy line between one soft, succulent cheek and her leg. She cried out, a husky moan that had him going in for more. He pressed his mouth against all that delicious wetness between her legs, lapping up the evidence of her first orgasm. She trembled, quivering with each lick, each kiss, each caress of his mouth. He broke contact to issue an instruction. "Spread your legs wider," he told her, "so I can bury my face in your beautiful pussy. Think you can come again? This time on my face, preferably."

"I don't know. But I'm willing to try," she answered, craning her neck to fix him with a naughty, mischievous grin as she planted her feet farther apart, flattening her back more, the position giving him unfettered access.

"That's the spirit," he said, returning to feast on her, licking and lapping her up. She didn't hold back, she didn't mute herself. She was loud, she was hungry, she called out his name, she called out God's name, she cried *yes* over and over, and he knew that their chemistry was for the record books. That he would absolutely miss these moments, and all the other ones, too, when their brief affair reached its expiration date.

But now was not the time to linger on endings. He had an ending of another kind in mind. An epic finale he wanted to give to her.

She was close, judging from the cries she made, from the way she thrust wildly against his face, and from how her wetness coated his stubbled jaw. She was so slippery that he couldn't resist sliding a finger inside her, then another, his entire body sparking with desire as she went off like a shot, coming again. He could taste her climax, and it was a drug to him. A heady, beautiful drug that made his brain and body light up.

He slowed his movements, giving her pussy one last kiss before he pulled away to grab the condom.

Then he whipped his head around when he heard a high-pitched voice.

"Let's play on the swing set!"

Chapter Nineteen

He froze for a second at the sound of her neighbors heading into their backyard. A fence separated the yards, but there was no sound barrier.

She scurried inside, and he grabbed the condom and quickly followed her, slamming the door shut behind them.

The sexy moment had turned into an almost-got-caught-by-a-kid one. He eyed her up and down. Her shoulders were shaking with laughter. Damn, the way she laughed, with so much joy, so much exuberance, had his heart speeding into overdrive, and this time it wasn't from desire, or from the need to get away quickly. It was from the wish that this didn't have to end. All of these moments with her were among his happiest, and he hated to let them slip through his fingers, even though he knew they were cruising to the finish line. The end was necessary, though. He could never give her what she needed or what she deserved. Best to concentrate only on the here and now. He grabbed her hand and pulled her naked body against his, brushing her hair off her shoulder.

"I have a completely wild and crazy idea."

"What is it?"

He held up his hands, took a deep breath, and spoke as if presenting something out of left field. "Seeing as we've christened every couch, table, counter, and appliance in this house, how about we break in your bed?"

He expected a *no*, given how she'd reacted with surprise the last time he'd suggested they get outside their comfort zone with a visit to a bed. But she was all *yes* today, nodding, grasping his hand, and leading him into her bedroom. The room was pure Cara—a purple bedspread, pillows in red and silver, and framed photos covering every inch of her dresser.

But he stopped looking around when she lay down on the cover and parted her legs for him.

So vulnerable, so beautiful, so aroused.

A groan worked its way up his chest as he walked over to her.

"You're gorgeous, Cara. So gorgeous, and perfect, and beautiful," he said, bending his head to kiss her ankle, then her calf, then her thigh.

She trembled under his touch and raised her arms to reach for him. "So are you."

He rolled on the condom, lowered himself between those long, lovely legs, and slid into her.

At last. He was home.

She wrapped her legs around his hips, and he thrust into her. She kept her gaze pinned on him, and he didn't want to look away either.

He wanted to say something, to tell her something dirty, to say something filthy.

But words eluded him now as he drove into her and she roped her arms around his shoulders, her body still hot and sweaty from the sun, and soft and pliant from the two orgasms. She gave herself to him, arching into him, holding on tighter, digging her nails harder, and he loved every second of this reaction from her.

He felt it, too. He felt the difference. It wasn't just the mattress. He couldn't attribute the furious beating of his heart to the change of scenery.

It was her.

All her…and how he wanted more from her than he had a right to want. Because he knew with a bone-deep certainty that this was how it should be. This was how a man and a woman were meant to be. This kind of connection, this kind of intensity, this kind of deep, primal need.

God, he would miss this.

He would miss her.

She moved beneath him—sensual, wild, and free as she called out his name, clutched his shoulders, and held on tight as she came apart in his arms. Within seconds he followed her there, joining her in ecstasy, in a finish that felt different from the others.

He kissed her cheek, her eyelids, her sweet, sexy lips, then slipped away briefly to remove the condom.

"Bet you didn't know it was really a three orgasm special today," he said, flopping down next to her on the bed when he returned, and holding her in his arms, layering kisses on her belly, her shoulder, her neck.

She laughed, and ran her fingers from his ribs through the hair on his chest. He squirmed the slightest amount.

She arched an eyebrow. "Are you ticklish?"

He shrugged noncommittally. "Not much."

Her eyes lit up, sparkling with naughtiness. "You are," she said, enunciating each word, like she'd caught him in a big, fat fib.

"Fine," he said, heaving a sigh. "Maybe more than a little."

She dragged her fingers once more over the ticklish spot, and he laughed out loud this time.

"Ha. I have found your weakness."

He narrowed his eyebrows, fixing her with a serious stare. "Don't use it against me, or I'll be forced to give you more than three orgasms, and you know what happens to your brain after three orgasms."

"I do not know. Tell me," she said, snuggling up closer, fitting far too wonderfully in his arms.

"You won't be able think straight any more. It's a very serious condition," he said.

"I'm willing to suffer for that affliction."

"Maybe for our last time I'll go for four," he whispered softly, then planted a kiss on her forehead. She tensed in his arms, and he wished instantly he could take those words back. But yet, it was better to focus on the truth. Neither one of them needed to lose sight of reality.

They didn't have a future. They weren't a couple. They couldn't be anything more than this two-week affair. But he wanted one more special moment with her, and he planned to take it.

• • •

The words cut. *Last time*. They were a cruel reminder that the clock ticked ever closer to the end. She shouldn't be upset. She had signed up for this. She'd requested this damn affair. But now, she wanted more than an affair. Only today was clearly not the time to ask for it. Not when the man was very much living in the here and now.

This was going to be harder than she thought—laying her heart on the line for someone who'd been one hundred percent clear and then some that he didn't do relationships.

Even though surely it had to mean something that they'd finally slept together in a bed? She could write it off as an escape from the neighbor's eyes, and it *was* that. But it also felt like something more.

For the first time, it felt like making love.

"Hey," he said, sitting up in bed. "Let's take a shower. I can't promise you that your fantasy of finding me there is ever going to come true, because the reality is I'd much rather be pleasuring you than myself, but at least we can get cleaned up."

"Fair enough," she said, trying to stay rooted in the moment. Later, when she was alone, she'd devise a strategy. She'd need time and a plan to do this right. Especially since asking for more with him was such a risk—the ultimate risk to her own mapped-out life. So she kept her words to a minimum for now as they headed to the bathroom.

He turned on the shower then reached for her hand to bring her under the hot stream with him. The tenderness of his touch, and the gentle way he held her hand, nearly split her heart wide open. She was so ready to blurt it all out, to spill everything she was trying desperately to keep locked up safely in her chest until she knew what to do with it.

He wrapped his arms around her, layering kisses on her shoulders. She bit the inside of her lip to keep from speaking.

"Hey," he said, whispering softly as the water rained down. "I know we both turn into pumpkins or something when the auction comes around, but what would you think about us going to the wedding together this weekend?"

Her heart stopped. "Like a date? Like in public?"

She lifted her chin to face him. Water streaked down her nose, a bead dropping off and splashing on the tiled shower floor. He leaned forward and kissed her nose. It was so damn affectionate, and he probably had no clue what all this sweetness was doing to her.

"Yes. A date. It's not like we've done such a good job hiding the fact that we're into each other, so we might as well just go together," he said, turning her around so her back rested against his chest. He reached for the shampoo and lathered up her hair. She leaned into him, a soft sigh escaping her lips as he washed her hair. A hope for more. A wish for both the hot, wild times in the yard, on the car, in the hallway, and the sweet, quiet ones like these.

"I would like that," she said, then didn't say anything more. What she really wanted were less mixed signals. But in the absence of clear ones, she'd have to figure out the next steps on her own.

• • •

She didn't see Travis the next night. She had plans with her sister and her parents for a welcome back celebration at Stacy's house. True, her parents had only been in South Carolina for a few weeks, but she and her sister had bought balloons and hung them up in Stacy's kitchen, with help from Stacy's husband and their four-year-old son. Their parents got a huge kick out of the over-the-top decorations, then regaled them with tales of the latest antics of their East Coast grandchildren.

After the meal, her parents left first, yawning as they headed to the door, saying the time difference between coasts was dragging them down. Then it was Cara's turn to say goodnight, so she read a book to her nephew, tucked him in bed, and said good night to her sister's husband as he cleaned the kitchen.

Stacy walked her out and gave her a hug on the porch.

"It's getting hard to hug you. You're like a double wide," Cara joked.

"Watch it. Or I'll add bleach to your shampoo when you're not looking, and you'll wake up with Bozo the clown hair."

Cara shuddered playfully as she left, then walked down the stone path in Stacy's front yard.

She opened the gate, and started to close it behind her, when she stopped. Night had fallen, and stars winked on and off in the sky. She gazed heavenward, hunting for the constellations she recognized.

The Jalapeno Dipper. Orion's Suspenders. And Cleopatra.

She flashed back to that night outside Becker's bar when Travis had renamed the stars. She'd scurried away from him then, doing everything to eradicate him from her mind. She'd had no luck though. And, as it turned out, her brilliant strategy to get him out of her system through a steady diet of mind-blowing sex had failed miserably, too.

She was no closer to getting over him. In fact, the opposite was true.

She wanted more of him.

She tore her gaze away from the endless star-spangled sky to the white fence her fingers were wrapped around.

A white picket fence.

Everything she thought she'd wanted.

And right then, with the clarity of the brightest star in the sky, she knew she had to let it go. She had to give up the dream. She'd found something she wanted more than her carefully detailed and neatly planned blueprint for happiness. She wanted Travis, and she'd have to find a way to meet him in the middle.

Chapter Twenty

As the sun rose, Cara called up the message from Joe. From her safe zone under her purple cover, she took a deep breath, clicked open his last email, and began typing.

> *"Thank you so much for the lovely dinner, and while I had a wonderful time, I need to decline our second date. You're a fantastic guy, so please don't think it's you. The problem is me, and my affections are elsewhere."*

She wanted to be direct, but kind. She hoped this note fit that bill.

An entire squadron of nerves took flight in her belly, but she somehow found the courage to hit send. She was only sending an email, but as it traveled into cyberspace, hurtling on a path to Joe's inbox, it felt like freedom from her own plans.

But it was fear, too. Fear of the great unknown. But you

had to let go before you could move forward. You had to give up the safety net before you went for what you wanted.

She wasn't sure how to navigate the *what's next* in her life without a roadmap.

But she'd figure it out soon enough. Probably today, in fact, since she had a wedding to attend.

• • •

Travis sneaked a quick peek at the time on his watch. The clock was ticking, and he had to hit the road to make it to the wedding.

But he had a client to calm down.

Hunter slammed the cards on the oak table at the private business club in Napa. He jammed his hands in his hair, plowing them through like bulldozers.

Travis had seen this before. This kind of frustration, from Hunter and from others like him—guys with lots of spare change. 'Course, that was his whole card-playing client list—high rollers. Venture capitalists, vineyard owners, real-estate developers—they turned to him in the first place because they had money to gamble. That was a blessing and a curse.

Hunter was the wildest of the lot. Like a caged lion in a zoo, he paced around the table, back and forth, back and forth. "What the hell just happened? How did I lose that much money?"

The room had been vacated. Travis had told the other gamblers to take five.

A vein pulsed in Hunter's neck. The man was close to snapping. He'd had two nines a few minutes ago. It was a good hand, but not nearly good enough for what he'd been wagering. Hunter had called Travis after the first hand of the game had gone bust, pretty much begging him to come by. Travis had been hoping the man was ready to have the apron strings cut. No such luck. So Travis dropped in and gave him a solid pep talk, but the advice had fallen by the wayside when the game turned heated. Travis swore he'd seen the dollar signs multiplying in Hunter's eyes as the pot swelled. The guy was rich, but he still hated losing money.

"Seriously. What happened?" Hunter asked, practically vibrating with negative ions. "Just tell me," he gritted out.

Calling on his best calm voice, the one he used not only with his card-playing clients but also in the firehouse, Travis prepared to lay it out for him. "Do you really want to know?"

"Yes." Hunter crossed his arms over his chest as he bit off the one-word answer.

"It's simple. You got too cocky. Too confident. You forgot the rules of the road," he said, opting for directness because he knew that was what Hunter needed. He was one of the few clients who'd been with Travis for several years. He still hadn't learned to rein in his childish desire to win big. This was Travis's specialty, though. He knew how to keep every emotion in check.

"But isn't that what the game is about? To go all in?"

"Yes and no," Travis answered. "This is not your livelihood, man. Even if it were, you'd need better control. But it's not. You play for fun. And you're not having fun when you lose this big. And you always lose big when you don't follow the plan."

Hunter sighed in frustration, and then cursed under his breath. "Shit."

"You're like this cleanup hitter who swings for the

fences every time. The opposing teams know you can't resist a fastball down the middle, so you swing every time and you miss. You need to play poker like you invest in the tech companies. You study the companies, you analyze their P and Ls, you know what you're getting into. You need to bring that to the game. You need to stop making decisions based on your emotions."

That approach had served Travis well in life and love. He'd studied the risks of relationships and analyzed the pros and cons. He knew when to hold and when to fold. Like with Cara. Even if some part of him craved more with her, he had to lean on the analytical side of his mind. That was the side that protected him from loss. He wanted Hunter to do the same when it came to poker.

Hunter nodded several times as the advice seemed to register. "You're right," he admitted.

"If you could do that, you wouldn't need me anymore, and I'd really like you to not need me, because that means I'll have finally done my job and taught you something," he said, clasping his hand on the man's shoulder. "Got it?"

"Got it," Hunter said with a nod.

"Now, I need to go to my buddy's wedding. You," he said, clasping his hands on Hunter's shoulders and staring him square in the eyes, "are going to master this."

"I am," he said with a nod.

Travis sure hoped so. He wanted to see the man act with his head, not his heart. The heart led to trouble, and no one needed trouble in his life.

. . .

"You look perfect."

Cara was the first bridesmaid to issue the declaration as the bride swiveled around to show off her attire. Megan had zipped up the back of Jamie's dress, and earlier in the day Cara's sister had transformed Jamie's long blond locks into a gorgeous French twist that made her look both classy and utterly sexy on her wedding day.

The dress was simple and elegant, with cap sleeves, a fitted bodice boasting a string of delicate beads, and an A-line skirt.

"I second it. You are gorgeous," Megan chimed in. "Now, look in the mirror, and prepare to be astonished."

Megan guided her to the full-length mirror behind the door in Jamie's bedroom, where they were helping the bride prep for her big day.

Jamie's eyes widened to moon-size and she clasped a hand over her lips.

Megan beamed. "Your dress is perfect. Everything is perfect."

Jamie nodded and swallowed visibly, as if she were holding back a tear. "I love it," she whispered reverently.

"No crying," Cara said, wagging a finger at the bride. "We can't have you messing up your makeup an hour before you say *I do*."

"I know, I know," Jamie said in a thin voice as she sucked in her breath and waved a hand in front of her made-up face. She flashed a bright smile. "There. It's all under control."

Jamie's phone rang from her small clutch purse on the bed, a high-pitched bell sounding. "My sister. She's overseeing the flowers," she said as she grabbed it and walked into the living room.

Cara glanced at the time. "As soon as she's done with her call we should go."

Megan nodded, and then plopped down on the edge of the bed. "Sorry. I'm just tired these days," she said, her hands resting on her belly.

"I think it's permissible to be tired, considering you're baking a person in your belly," Cara said.

Megan smiled, then cleared her throat. "So I hear you and Travis are going together today. Well, meeting up there, since we're going with Jamie in the limo."

Cara blushed but nodded. "Yes. Sort of like a date," she said. Then she raised her chin higher, owning it. Megan knew they'd dated on and off; she knew they were having a *thing*. They were all adults. She didn't need to act coy. "Actually, exactly like a date."

Megan's features lit up, a wide smile spreading across her face. "It's about time," she said with a quirk in her lips.

Cara shrugged. "I don't know that it'll amount to more than a date."

"Do you want it to be more?" Megan asked, crossing her legs and kicking her sandaled foot back and forth. She'd chosen a pale yellow dress for today; Cara had opted for peach. Jamie said she wanted her friends to pick their own colors. Jamie didn't call them bridesmaids. She and Smith had chosen not to have specific titles for everyone. They'd simply asked their closest friends to stand with them.

"I do want it to be more. I have no idea if he does though. He's not the easiest guy to read," Cara said, then stopped and quickly corrected herself. "Actually, he's quite easy to read because he's so direct. What I mean is I have no idea if he'd ever want more than just one last date."

Megan smoothed her hands over her skirt. "He's a bit rigid, isn't he?"

Cara laughed, but it came out a bit more like a scoff. "Yeah, that kind of describes him."

"Listen. I don't know if Travis is a 'more' kind of guy, but all I can say is when he came by my house to get flowers for you, that was a big tip-off. He's never done that before for a woman."

Cara's heart beat harder. "They were lovely flowers."

"And he asked me for the recipe for my cookies," she added.

"Well, that was over a bet he lost," she admitted with a shrug. "But they were amazing cookies."

"And he brags constantly about the things you've taught Henry. And how he thinks you're great at everything. Cooking, dogs, making him laugh…"

"Okay, now I'm going to blush even more," Cara said, waving her hand in the air, as if she needed to cool off.

Megan rose and draped an arm around Cara, squeezing her shoulder. "It's not as if he confides in me, but I think I know my brother pretty well. He's been changing because of you, Cara. I can see it. Heck, Becker can even see it. And when a man's friends can pick up on that, you know it's real."

"It is real," she said softly. A butterfly flapped happily inside her chest. Maybe she wasn't so crazy for coming up with her plan.

In the forty-eight hours since he'd asked her to be his wedding date, she'd mulled over the right words, the right time, and the right way to put her heart on the line.

She'd logged a few hours on the elliptical processing her options.

She'd spent time walking Violet discussing the details with her dog.

She'd even jotted down a few notes in between her training sessions.

After all the time she'd spent with Travis in the last few weeks... No, she corrected herself, after *all these years*, she knew what she was feeling. Knew it cold.

Besides, she was pretty damn sure she wasn't flying solo in the feelings department. From the sweet words he'd said, to the times they'd shared, and even to making love in a bed at last, somewhere along the way this fling had changed for her, and she was willing to bet the rules of the road had changed for him, too.

She wanted this date at the wedding to be the start of something, not the end of it.

Maybe that was all she truly needed to say to him, but she also knew how very important the fireman's auction was to him. He'd come to her for help. He'd come to her because he had a mission and a goal. She wanted to show she understood him and supported those dreams, and the place where they came from. Because they came from the very spot that had made it so hard for him to let anyone in. He'd let *her* in, though, so she wanted to honor that in the way she told him how she felt.

The prospect of rejection terrified her, but not as much as she loathed the notion of him walking across the stage tomorrow night and another woman winning him.

"Here's my plan," Cara said, and then laid it out in detail.

Megan gave a huge thumbs up.

All that was left was the execution.

Chapter Twenty-One

His mother fiddled with his bow tie, straightening it. He huffed out a sigh. "Mom," he said.

"Travis," Robert chided as he watched from the kitchen doorway. "This is your mom's only chance to neaten a bow tie. Let her enjoy it. Well, unless you're the best man at your sister's wedding."

His mom's eyes lit up.

"Yes. More bow-tie fiddling," Travis said. "I can't wait. Besides, there's no best man today. And no bridesmaids. I told you that before." He wasn't a huge fan of weddings, but admittedly, Smith and Jamie's "all our friends will stand with us" philosophy was a cool idea.

"Let me fiddle," she said. Travis relented, letting his mom smooth her hands over his shoulders now. "You look very handsome. And I can't wait 'til you're the best man again."

"Always the best man, never the groom," he said, standing taller as he reminded her of his always single status.

His mom shot him a rueful smile. "I know how you feel about relationships. Now be on your way. Henry only has six more months of being a lone grandchild before I have a human one, too," she said, as she grabbed a tennis ball from the living room coffee table, and held it up high for Henry. The dog sat on the living room carpet, wagging his tail and panting eagerly for the ball.

Travis held out a hand. "Wait. You need to check this out. This is the big finish for the auction."

He showed them the dog's special trick, and Henry executed it perfectly. Like a pro.

From the doorway, Robert slow clapped. "Very impressive. He'll be great on stage. He is a certified chick magnet for sure."

"Yup. He graduated with full honors from the class in How to Reel Them In," he said, handing the dog back to his mom.

"I'll say," she said. "Now, go have fun."

Travis left, hopped into his truck, and drove to the vineyard where he'd be meeting Cara. When he parked at Ode Vines and stepped out of the car, his heart beat faster than he was used to. A strange prickling sensation traveled down his spine.

Like spiders inching along his back.

His stomach seemed to flip, ever so briefly, and he stared at his midsection as if he could ask his body what the hell was going on. Were those nerves? Nah. He couldn't possibly have nerves. This wasn't his wedding.

But as he shut the door to his truck and crunched across the gravel parking lot, scanning for Cara near the entryway, those nerves seemed hell-bent on having their way with him.

He reached the stone path leading into the winery and heard his name

"Travis!"

He spun around, the late afternoon sun blinding him. He slapped his hand above his eyes to shield them from the rays and hunted for the voice that was making his heart dance furiously in his chest. The only voice that could do that to him.

"I forgot my purse. Just grabbing it from the limo," he heard Cara say. Then, he spotted a long, gleaming black bullet of a car—the luxury vehicle that the ladies had ridden over in. As he crossed the parking lot, he could see clearly again.

The world around him narrowed to one single color.

Peach.

He'd never been jealous of an item of clothing before. Not until he saw the way the peach dress hugged her body, clinging so deliciously to her full breasts, her slim waist, and those fantastic legs. The dress stopped at her knees, offering him a fantastic view of her calves.

She was stunning.

He walked to her.

"You're beautiful," he said preemptively. It was his natural gut reaction. She was beauty from head to toe, in every way. He was a lucky son of a bitch to have this woman on his arm, and he intended to savor every single second of this last night out with her. After this affair ended, maybe even one day soon, some bastard would win her for good and take her home every night. That image was a strange black cloud that appeared out of nowhere, briefly enveloping him in its awfulness.

He blinked, if he could shake away the horrible notion of someone else gazing at her the way he looked at her.

"So are you," she said, then she gestured to the winery. "We should go in."

The door to the backseat of the limo was still open, so he reached behind her to shut it. As he held out an arm, he could see a flash of his future, closing the car door for her, taking her out, having her by his side at these events. But then, just as quickly as that reel played, his arms felt trapped, pinned down and tied up by those possibilities. They weren't in his game plan. They led to hurt, to pain, and to risks he couldn't let himself take.

He was a guy for the present, not for the future.

He tried his best to erase those images of her and him together. Delete them from his mental files. But his damn brain was being tricked by how goddamn beautiful she was right now.

"So, um, you look great," he said as they neared the stone path leading to the big main doors of the winery. He realized he'd already said that. Why the hell was he repeating himself?

"So do you," she said, and it seemed she'd said that, too. Perhaps she was suffering from the same bout of tongue-tied-ness.

"Damn weddings," he mumbled.

"What do you mean?" she asked, tilting her head.

"They're just so…" he said, but couldn't finish the thought, so he let his voice trail off.

"Yeah, I know what you mean," she said in a soft, wistful tone, then squeezed his arm tighter. His heart thumped harder, and he wished that he didn't like it so much that she simply *got* him. That he didn't have to explain everything. She knew what he meant. Weddings were just so damn hard. The promises of commitment, the way two people could look at each other and see forever. His chest clenched, and a hot burst of high-octane dread coursed through him as they reached the door.

He didn't feel at home in his own damn body, and he couldn't figure out why. So he turned to the one thing he knew for certain. Contact with her. He pulled her away from the door, and around to the side of the building, then tugged her into a quiet doorway.

"What is it?" she asked. "The wedding starts in a few minutes."

He didn't answer her with words. He held her face and dropped a quick kiss to her lips. Hers were soft, and she tasted so damn sweet, like lip gloss, and the way he imagined the word "pretty" would taste. A soft, sexy sigh escaped her lips as she melted into his arms. She wedged her gorgeous body against his, fitting so perfectly alongside him. He gathered her closer, roping his arms around her, kissing her more deeply and letting her feel how utterly turned on he was by her.

"Do you have any idea how much I want you right now?" he asked, and finally, he was on sure footing again. The way their bodies were in sync made much more sense than this topsy-turvy day. Everything else was a jumble, but *this* — the pure physical — was as simple as knowing when to hold and when to fold. He vastly preferred the things he understood.

She wriggled against his erection. "I do know."

"Damn, now I'm gonna be hard during the wedding. Not good."

"Want me to talk about sweaty basketball players so it goes down?" she said with a naughty smile, and he laughed then let his eyes drift to the front of his pants.

"Admittedly, that image helped a bit. But being next to you isn't going to help. I'll be thinking about you the whole time, and how I want you. How many ways I want you," he said, lowering his voice.

She pretended to swat him, but the sexy smile on her face told him that she liked his words, so he kept going. They were so easy to say to her. "You look more than beautiful, and you make it too difficult to keep my hands off you," he said. He couldn't resist raining down compliments on this woman. Or touching her, for that matter, so he returned to her lips, kissing her softly, tracing his tongue along the sweet curve of her top lip, then nibbling on the bottom one. Soon, she placed her hands on his chest and gently pushed him away.

"Travis, you're turning me on far too much. I can't stand there all worked up and wanting you as they get married."

"Why not?"

"Because," she said emphatically. "Now, let's go to the ceremony before we're too hot and bothered for our own good."

"I like hot and bothered," he whispered, as she led him around to the vineyard.

Twenty minutes later, he was surrounded by the fragrance of grapes and the twisting branches of vines as Smith pledged to love Jamie for the rest of his life, and as Jamie repeated those same words back to him. Even though weddings weren't his thing, and he would never ever be the man in front of everyone making those promises, he couldn't help but be happy for his friend. Smith had been crazy about Jamie for a long time, and they'd been friends for years before they finally admitted how they felt.

"Do you, Smith, pledge to love, honor, and cherish this woman for the rest of your life?"

The deep voice of the justice of the peace boomed over the crowd, and Travis hazarded a glance at his date, who stood next to him. Her eyes were fixed on the couple, her lips parted slightly, so much restrained emotion on her face, it was as if she were one step away from crying. As Smith said yes and clasped Jamie's hands in his, a tear slid down Cara's cheek.

Before Travis could think better of it, he brushed it off, then threaded his fingers through hers. He hated to see a woman cry. He had ever since he'd seen far too much of it from his mother. He'd do just about anything to make a woman stop crying.

Especially over something like a wedding.

Chapter Twenty-Two

It had to be a sign.

Why else would he hold her hand during the wedding vows? Her heart was beating outside her body, and she was more certain than ever that her feelings were requited. From the way he curled his fingers through hers, to how he gently brushed away a tear, every gesture told her that he was ready for *more*.

Surely, this was a two-way street. Surely, there was more to them than great sex. She didn't know if she could wait 'til tomorrow night. He squeezed her fingers harder and shifted his body closer. She fought hard to rein in a crazy grin. There was no way he'd touch her like this, at this time, if he wasn't ready to change his stripes.

"And now may we have the rings," the officiant asked.

She tensed briefly in anticipation as she turned to watch Chance lope down the makeshift aisle like a pro. Chance trotted happily, not speeding, and not lollygagging either, until he reached Smith and Jamie, who both patted his head at the same time.

Chance didn't even need to be told to sit. He simply parked his rear on the ground and puffed out his chest, like a gymnast who'd nailed the landing.

"Good boy," Smith said as he reached for the rings from the leather pouch. The dog lay down as the bride and groom finished their vows.

"I now pronounce you husband and wife. You may kiss the bride," the officiant intoned. That was Cara's cue to call Chance over. With a low whistle and a clap, she brought him to her side as Smith and Jamie kissed. Everyone clapped and cheered, and joy floated through the air, infecting all of them. Even Travis, who brushed his lips against her cheek in a soft kiss. Her heart began to pirouette. He'd never kissed her like that in front of their friends. The night at the club was different. That was dirty, sexy, hot kissing. This was sweet, possessive, romantic kissing for all the world to see.

Twenty-four hours from now seemed too far away to tell him how she felt. She was ready to tell him any second.

Then it hit her—she had a mission to take care of *this* second.

So she tabled all her thoughts of tomorrow to focus on the here and now, and the little bitty problem she faced. She didn't have a car. She'd ridden with Jamie and Megan in the limo. But she was supposed to bring Chance to the dog hotel where he'd be boarding, since Smith and Jamie were heading to Mexico for a honeymoon the morning after the fireman's auction.

"Travis," she said, her voice low and worried. "Would you mind terribly driving Chance and me to the Doggie B and B?"

His lips curved up. "You going home with Chance instead of me?"

She laughed. "Maybe. He is quite cuddly. And I hear he doesn't hog the sheets."

"Hey. I'm not a sheet-hogger either," he said. "And I will even prove it to you tonight."

Her damn heart started skipping. Okay, this was going far too well. He was giving her nothing but positive signs. He hadn't spent the night at all during their affair. The fact that he wanted to tonight was another brick in the foundation of her certainty.

She gathered up the dog, let Jamie and Smith give him a quick good-bye hug, then headed to Travis's truck. Chance sprawled out on the backseat, and they scurried the big guy off to the local dog B and B, a true haven for the vacationing beasts, since it boasted free run of the house for canines who were lucky enough to enjoy a cageless stay.

"That place is nicer than most hotels I've stayed at," Travis said, pointing his thumb at the red door as the proprietor swung it shut behind them.

"Nothing but the best for Chance, and I'm sure you'd do the same for Henry, especially since he's definitely going to nab you top honors tomorrow night," she said, nudging him with her elbow as they returned to his car and buckled in.

He arched an eyebrow as he put the key in the ignition. "Yeah? You think it's just the dog?"

She shook her head and placed her hand on his cheek. "Nope. The dog and the man are the full package."

He looked her in the eyes, his gaze serious. He parted his lips but said nothing at first. Then he cleared his throat. "You say the nicest things to me. You really think we're going to win tomorrow?"

She nodded, feeling a bit like she had an ace up her sleeve. "I can pretty much guarantee it."

"It'll all be because of you. Hell, without you my hair would be a mess and my dog would be humping legs."

"Speaking of," she said, letting her hand trail down his cheek, to his jaw, to his chest. Touching him like this turned her on.

"You want to hump my leg?"

She laughed. "No. But you're getting warm."

He groaned and gripped her hand. "What you do to me, woman," he said, his voice low and husky, sending a hot shiver down her spine.

"You do the same to me."

"Okay. You're killing me. I'm not going to be able to make it through the reception now."

"So let's visit Miner's Road on the way back," she suggested, feeling naughty and daring. Feeling so damn confident that everything was going her way.

"We haven't been to Miner's Road since after prom," he said, backing up and pulling out of the lot. "And that's about to change right now."

Miner's Road was a quiet street that dead-ended at a trailhead to the woods that had been closed down a few years ago. The hiking path was deemed too dangerous. But that only meant the end of the road was perfect for lovers.

He turned onto the curving road back to the winery as twilight sprinkled across the sky. She ran her hand along his leg as he drove. His breath hitched, and his throat made a rumbly sound. She traveled up to his erection, cupping him through his pants.

"I hate the thought of you walking around all night like this."

"As do I," he said.

"And I bet you'd be equally frustrated if you knew how I'd be walking around."

"How?"

With her free hand, she inched up the skirt of her dress, revealing her thighs, then her panties.

He nearly swerved off the road when he saw the white lace.

"Cara," he said, and she loved that certain moments rendered the man incapable of saying more than her name. She leaned her head back, played with the waistband of her panties, and whispered, "Say my name again."

"Cara," he said roughly, as he made a sharp right for their detour when they reached the lover's lane.

She dropped her hand inside her panties. "Do you want me?"

"You know I do," he rasped out as he gunned the motor. "You know I want you more than anything."

He reached the end of the quiet road and cut the engine. He turned off the lights, moved out of the driver's seat and into hers, quickly shifting her on top of him.

"I don't want to mess up that pretty hair," he said, gently brushing his hand along her chignon. "So you're going to need to ride me."

"I believe I'd be amenable to that," she said as she slid off her panties. "Seems I'm all ready."

He grabbed a condom from his pocket and pushed down his briefs. "Funny. Me, too."

She bunched up her skirt at her waist and straddled him.

She gripped his shaft, thrilling at the instant reaction her touch elicited. He closed his eyes and groaned. She stroked him, savoring the feel of his rock hard cock. A fierce sense of possession wove through her—the deep belief that he was hers, and she was his, and that the two of them simply belonged together.

Their connection might have started here, on this road, long ago, but it ran deeper now and reached farther, stretching into a future together. She rolled the condom on him and lowered herself onto his erection, sparks of heat roaring through her as he buried himself in her. He groaned and gripped her ass, moving her up and down on him. Space was at a premium in his vehicle, but she didn't mind being snug, her knees tucked up, taking him.

"Come closer," he whispered. "Let me feel you."

She lowered her chest to his, and they were gazing at each other, an intense line of connection like an invisible thread between them. "Hi," she said, moving up and down on him, each thrust making her bolder, giving her confidence in the possibility of *them*.

"Hi," he said, and he cupped her face. "Hi, you absolutely beautiful woman. I can't stop looking at you."

"So don't," she said, rocking faster, more fiercely, as they moved together in rhythm.

"I won't," he said, and his voice touched down deep inside her, setting off a chain reaction, pleasure surging through her, running over her skin, taking hold of her body. She blazed with need for him. With longing.

With love.

"I don't want this to stop," she moaned, and she wasn't

talking about the orgasm that started to overtake her body.

"I don't either."

She moved on him until he came too.

Maybe he did want the same things. All of them.

• • •

Two hours later, she was feeling pretty good. It was every-thing—from the sex, to all the ways he'd touched her, to the laugher, to their friends, to the love that was simply in the air.

Oh and, yeah, this glass of champagne played a role too. The bubbles tickled her nose as she took another sip. The waiters had poured the drink freely, and it was time for toasts. Jamie's parents had toasted, her sister had said a few words, then Smith's dad joined in, and even the reserved Becker had spoken about how glad he was to see the two of them together.

Cara held out her glass to Travis and clinked with him as Becker finished with a hearty "Congrats!" then handed the mic back to Jamie.

"How about Cara?"

Cara blinked and turned around to find Jamie, staring at her from the middle of the reception room, waving her over. "You found our dog, and the dog brought us together for real!"

Cara laughed, and shrugged.

Travis nudged her on. "Go say a few words. Make fun of Smith."

But that wasn't her style. She wasn't a roaster at toasts. She weaved through the crowd under the twinkling lights and took the mic. She scanned the room quickly, cataloguing a sea of friends, of family, of all the people in Hidden Oaks who she adored. This was her town. Her home. The place where she was meant to be. Destiny or fate had brought her from Nevada to here years ago, and the need to be close to her family had called her back last year. Now, as she rested her gaze on Travis, she knew that all she wanted was in this town—she'd waited and longed for a love like this.

And it had been him, right here, all these years.

She didn't plan on blurting out her feelings in front of everyone. That would be the height of tacky to steal the floor at a friend's wedding, but she could start.

"I just wanted to say that Jamie and Smith have always been perfect for each other. I've known that. Anyone who spent any time with them could see it. In fact, I even told Smith a few years ago that it was obvious that he was madly in love with her," Cara said, locking eyes with the bride and groom, and they knew exactly what she was talking about— those two dates she went on with Smith that made it clear to her that he was hung up on another woman. That was fine by her, since she and Smith were better off as friends, and since she too was hung up on someone else. Always had been, ever since their first date in high school. "In any case, when Smith asked me last year to help him find a dog for Jamie, that's when I knew it was true love for both of them."

A chorus of oohs and ahs emanated from the attendees. Smith tugged Jamie in for a kiss.

"See?" She pointed at the bride and groom, locked in a kiss. "This is what I'm talking about, right?" Cara tossed the question out to the crowd, and was met with a collective *yes*. "And my take is this—sometimes a dog can bring two people together." Her gaze stopped to settle on Travis, hooked into his from across the room. Her heart filled with warmth; hope and nerves flooded her bloodstream. Still, she pressed on. The undercurrent of her toast was for him. "I suppose a dog, like Chance, or even a pair of dogs, can kind of be matchmakers. I like to think they have a way of bringing two people who were meant to be together even closer. Here's to dogs and love."

Travis tipped his water glass to her, the crowd raised their drinks, and Jamie thrust her champagne flute high in the air. "I think we need to dance," the bride declared.

The DJ took the cue, cranking up some music, and Cara set down the mic on the table and returned to Travis.

"Want to dance?" he asked, and she said yes. They moved to the dance floor and swayed. "Nice speech, by the way."

His gorgeous blue eyes, like an azure stream, never strayed from hers. In his eyes, she saw such passion, such honesty, such vulnerability. She wanted to be the woman he trusted, the woman he was willing to make a go of it for, because he was the man for her. Screw waiting. She didn't need to surprise him at the auction to let him know how she felt. There was no time like the present.

"It was about you," she said softly.

"What?" He tilted his head to the side, as if he hadn't quite heard her.

"The part about two people who were meant to be together. That was you and me. Us, Travis, us," she said, and it was as if she'd swallowed a dose of sheer terror, and it was coursing through her body right now. But on the other side was hope, and possibility, and all her dreams coming true.

She shoved her fears behind her and didn't look back.

"It was?" he asked, furrowing his brow.

What the hell? Was this complex math to him? "Yes," she said in a clear, firm voice. "It was about you. You didn't realize that?"

He shook his head. "No. I thought it was about Smith and Jamie," he said, slicing a hand through the air as if he could eliminate the possibility that she'd been talking about him.

Okay, time to spell it out. "Travis, I'm just going to say it. I thought I could get you out of my system with this arrangement we had, but I can't and there's a reason. Because you're not supposed to be out of it. You're supposed to be in it. And in my life. I thought I had to make all the smart and wise choices, because I didn't come from a place of smart and wise choices. But I've learned that some things can't be planned perfectly, and maybe it's better if they're not planned. So I'm letting go of all those things I told myself I had to have, because I don't want to lose you." She gripped his shoulders the whole time, needing something solid to hold as she poured out her heart. "And I know you don't believe in serious relationships, but I'm not asking for the white picket fence, or a ring. I tried to plan my life down to the day, and I'm not doing that anymore. All I'm asking is if you'd like to try something more. If you'd like for this fling to be more than dog training and sex, because I feel so much more for you. And I would really like to bid on you tomorrow night, and take you off the market, because I can't stand the thought of any other woman having you," she said, taking a breath after all those words tumbled out.

"Because I am in love with you."

Chapter Twenty-Three

His ears rang.

Blood pounded in his head.

This wasn't possible. There was no way she could have just said *that*.

Those were words he'd never heard before. They were words he didn't *want* to hear. They didn't fit his plan. They didn't adhere to the rules he lived by. They threw him out of whack, like a washing machine tossed into an unbalanced spin cycle.

Up was down. Left was right. The room spun wildly out of control.

He said the first words that came to his head. "You don't mean that."

She narrowed her eyes and shot him a strange look. "I do mean it. Why else would I say it? Do you think I just go around saying things I don't mean?"

He shook his head, and his skull felt heavy, like there

was water in his brain, slogging around. The melody from the pop song played in the background. He barely even recognized it as the tune they'd been dancing to seconds ago. The words seemed to be sung from a distant planet.

Hell, he felt like he was on Jupiter right now. Nothing made sense. From the way his heart had jumped around in his chest when he first saw her tonight, to how much he'd enjoyed the simple and easy way they'd spent their evenings—cooking and talking and christening new surfaces in and out of their homes—even to how he'd felt in her bed the other night. None of those made a lick of sense either.

But maybe... Were they part and parcel of why she thought she was in love with him? Were all those topsy-turvy, kaleidoscopic feelings that knotted up his chest some sort of sign that he'd fallen, too?

No.

No way.

He dismissed the ridiculous notion of love as quickly as it had arrived. If he put stock in such crazy ideas, he'd be in big trouble. Especially because his stupid heart was trying to talk him out of what he was about to say.

But this wasn't a moment for the heart. The head had to stay in control.

"No, I just didn't think that's what this was about," he said softly, gesturing from her to him and back. As if reminding her of the deal could erase what she'd just said. "You didn't want anything more from me. You made it clear that day in the park that I could never be the man for you. Hell, you said it at my house too when you proposed this whole dog training and sex idea. I thought we were supposed to stick to the plan."

She breathed in hard, as if she were trying to suck in all the air through a straw. "You're right. That's what we planned. But things changed for me. I thought they changed for you, too?"

They had. Oh hell, they had. But he couldn't let himself be guided by something as risky as emotions. Emotions were dangerous. Especially since they were already affecting her.

Her voice rose at the end of her question, quavering, and he fought every instinct to gather her in his arms and comfort her. He wouldn't give in, though, because he *had* to make her see where she'd gone off track. She might think she'd be content kicking their fling up a notch or two. But her happiness with that kind of relationship would soon fade. This woman deserved the world. She deserved a man who could truly give her all her dreams, not merely satisfy her compromises.

"Sure, things changed, but Cara, you deserve more than a guy like me. You might think you're in love, but—" he stopped to gesture wildly to the scene around them—all the dancing and the drinking and the laughing. "You're just saying that because of the wedding, because the sex is great, because you had a glass of champagne."

"Oh. Is that it?" she asked, her voice hard now.

"Of course. Weddings do that to people. They work their voodoo magic, their smoke and mirrors," he said, layering on reason on top of reason to prove his point, to protect her from this risk she wanted to take. Hell, she reminded him of Hunter now, swinging for the fences, falling in love with the pot, not the hand. He had to treat her the same way as a client going off the deep end. He didn't let Hunter deviate from the roadmap; he had to protect Cara from too many emotions, too. He would not let the strange, funny, foreign things he'd been feeling when he was with her derail him. He'd had a plan since he was a kid. He'd seen how love and the loss of it could tunnel a hole in a family. He'd spent the last twenty years since his father's death learning how to manage risks, studying, analyzing, and figuring out precisely when, how, and where to take them and how to avoid them. Nowhere in that plan was there room for a woman falling in love with him, and certainly there wasn't room for him falling in love with her either.

She narrowed her eyes. "You're saying I feel this way because of a wedding?"

He swallowed dryly. He hated to say the next words, but he had to do this for her sake. She was better off not being in love with a man who couldn't return the sentiment. Regret washed over him, but he knew that as hard as these words were to say, he had to give voice to them. He had to let her go so she could have the life she craved. That life was not ever going to be with him. "We were just having a good time. We had a good time tonight, and on Miner's Road, and here at the reception. The whole thing. It was a good time."

"Yeah. A good time," she said, repeating him, but the words came out like a bite and he practically felt the teeth marks in his skin. She stepped away from him and crossed her arms. "You're right, Travis. It's just the champagne, it's just the sex, it's just the wedding. It couldn't possibly be anything else. Because I couldn't possibly fall in love with someone who would belittle my feelings like you just did. I hope you have a good night now. Excuse me. I'm going to the ladies room."

She turned on her heel and cut through the sea of friends

and family dancing with each other, old couples swaying to the music, young couples rocking it out, Smith and Jamie laughing and kissing, the gray-haired woman who owned the coffee shop shaking her hips with her equally-silver-haired husband, even his fellow firefighter Jackson dancing with the town's librarian, Kelly. Everyone was together, and he wasn't even truly here.

He could barely figure out how to move his feet, how to take a step, what to do next.

All he knew was that risks like this didn't add up. They didn't pan out.

Even though the evidence all around on the dance floor proved the opposite. But he put on his blinders, not wanting to see what was in front of him.

A few minutes later, he headed out of the reception room, across the hallway, and to the ladies' room door. The least he could do was apologize for making her feel so bad. He said her name softly. He didn't hear anything. He pushed open the door. "Cara?"

But her name simply echoed across the tiles. He looked down, to see if he could spot her shoes underneath the stalls. No one was there.

He turned around and nearly bumped into Becker, who'd just come in from outside. "Have you seen Cara?"

Becker nodded, and his eyes looked sad. Wait. That was wrong. It wasn't sadness Travis saw in them. It was disappointment.

He'd seen it from his mentor, from his mother, and even from his dad when he was younger and had messed up. "She's leaving," Becker said, pointing his thumb to the door. "We just put her in the limo and the driver is going to take her home."

Something in his heart cratered, and he squeezed his eyes shut.

Then he took off for the door, pushed it open, and ran across the gravel in hot pursuit of the limo. The sleek black car was trudging slowly across the lot. He caught up in seconds; his volunteer gig as a fireman had its perks—a quick burst of speed. He banged on the black tinted window several times.

The car stopped, and he breathed out heavily. Then, the window lowered, but as it did, he realized he had no fucking clue what to say.

Cara's face appeared in the open window. Her lips were a tight line, but her blue eyes couldn't hide the hope she must be feeling.

The way he'd felt inside the reception was nothing compared to the complete and utter awareness of what an asshole he was about to be.

"I'm sorry," he muttered.

She shook her head. "Good-bye, Travis," she said, and raised the window.

Chapter Twenty-Four

His mom answered the door in her bathrobe. The stern but surprised look in her blue eyes told him that she hadn't been expecting him tonight.

His bow tie was gone, his shirt's top two buttons were undone, and all he wanted was his dog. Henry raced down the stairs and greeted Travis at the door, tail wagging. "Hey, buddy," he said, bending down to scoop him up in his arms.

Henry licked his cheek. Travis understood his dog. Henry made sense to him, Henry was easy to take care of, he responded, he listened, and Travis knew exactly what Henry needed at any time during the day. When the dog paced at the door, he needed to go outside; when he nosed the cupboard in the evening, he was hungry for dinner; when he pawed at his leash it was time for a walk.

Women, on the other hand, were more confusing than astrophysics.

"I didn't expect to see you until tomorrow morning," his

mom said. As she shut the door behind him, Travis crumpled onto the couch in the living room, slumping into a tuxedoed mess.

"Sorry. I thought I was going to be somewhere tonight but it didn't work out."

His mom sat across from him in a chair, studying him as if she could find in his expression the answer to his much-earlier-than-expected appearance. "Translation: You mean you were going to spend the night with Cara and now you're not, probably because you said something stupid."

His jaw dropped. "Mom! Why would you assume I said something stupid?"

"Because you're my son, and I know you. And I know Cara. And that means I can put two and two together."

He slouched deeper into the well-worn couch. He ran a hand through his hair. "It's not that simple. She wants a relationship and that's not what I do."

His mom nodded several times, then she narrowed her eyes. "What is it that you *do*, then?"

"Mom, don't act surprised," he said, scrubbing a hand across his jaw. "You know they're not my thing. Never have been. Not after what they did to you and Dad."

She arched an eyebrow. "What they did to your dad and me? Travis, does that even make sense to you?"

"Of course," he said, quickly before he could even think about the question.

"Well, think about it more seriously. Because it doesn't make a bit of sense to me. Relationships didn't *do* anything to your father and me. He died in an accident in the line of duty. Not because of a relationship. And I know you made a decision long ago, because of how deeply his death affected me, that you would protect yourself from relationships. All I can do is say the same thing to you that I said to your sister. I am sorry that his death took such a toll on me when you were younger."

She sat up tall in her chair, keeping her gaze firmly fixed on him. "But you know what? I got over it. And I'm glad I'm here. I'm glad I have my heart to love again." She tapped her chest, reminding him that her ticker still worked. "My heart is strong. Robert is amazing, and I am unbelievably happy with him. Yes, I was devastated when your father died, and for many years after. And yes, if I could redo those years, I would change many things. But the one thing I will not regret is that I didn't shut off my heart. If I had, I wouldn't have the life I have today," she said, sweeping her arm out to indicate her home and, down the hall, her sleeping husband. "When your father died, I had a hole in my heart, and missing him was terrible. But then, time healed it. Because that's what time does. I could have closed myself off from ever loving again. But that's the real death. I hope you realize that. It is so much worse to live without love."

Those last words were a sharp punch in the chest, stronger than the stinging slap he suspected Cara had wanted to give him when he chased after her in the limo and still couldn't reciprocate.

He looked at his mom, and then his eyes roamed the house, cataloguing all the evidence of how his mother had taken a chance on love again, even when she'd been dealt the worst hand of all. She still had the photos of their father, the pictures of their younger years, and then she had new images on the tables and the walls — ones of her family now. Of her and Robert, of Megan and Becker, even of Travis and Henry. He flashed back on the lean years, then the ones that followed, remembering all the times he'd spent with his mom and his stepdad, from the barbecues, to the dinners, to even just the average, ordinary days now when they took care of his dog.

He could feel something shift in his chest, like a brick moving to let sunlight into a darkened room. "I'm glad you have Robert now," he said softly. "I'm glad you're happy."

"I am, and maybe you can be, too."

"I am happy," he said, straightening his spine. "I have everything a man could want. Friends, family, a dog, a good job."

She nodded. "Right. You do. And you could have something even more amazing if you'd get out of your own way."

"What's that supposed to mean?"

She yawned, rose, and rumpled his hair. "It means, young man, that it has not gone unnoticed for the last ten years that you've been in love with one girl." She stood up and walked to her bedroom, waving once along the way.

His jaw hit the floor. He rubbed his knuckle against his ear. Surely he was hearing things. "What the hell was that about?"

Henry cocked his head to the side, one ear shooting up in answer. "Now I know she's crazy," he said to the dog, then leashed him up and headed to his truck. His mom was nuts. That was the craziest thing he'd ever heard. Besides, he didn't need anything more. He was blessed already, and life had treated him well lately. He didn't need to push his luck and ask for more. That's what always got his clients in trouble. That's where people got hurt in a fire, too, when they went back in to save the family photos, the mementos, that precious little thing they thought they couldn't live without.

He settled Henry into the passenger seat, then buckled himself in. He backed out of the driveway, turned onto the street, then drove out to the main drag.

As he headed home through the dark and quiet night, the calm descending over Hidden Oaks, he rewound to his mom's words, then returned to the things Cara had said to him, and finally he replayed the look on Becker's face. His chest tightened as all these thoughts and images collided in his head, and he tried to detach them from each other, and make sense of them.

But was there any way to truly make sense of all these bizarre feelings? Especially the way he felt when he was near Cara, that strange, funny sensation that was like his heart trying to do cartwheels. He shook his head as he turned onto the main street through town.

Man, he was going crazy trying to dissect this.

A yellow light streaked past him. His skin prickled, and his muscles tensed all over. A horn blared from another car. He slammed on his brakes, and the rear of his car fishtailed as he swerved out of the way of a white hatchback that had been hurtling toward him.

What the hell? Where had that car come from? The driver wasn't paying attention at all.

Then he noticed the light at the intersection.

His pulse sped to sprinter levels when he realized what he'd just done. He'd run the red light at the town square.

Henry cowered on the floor of the car. The near-collision had knocked him out of the front seat and onto the floor. The poor guy was shaking. Quickly, Travis pulled to the side of the road and cut the engine. He reached for Henry and held him close. "You okay, buddy?" he asked, stroking Henry's fur. The dog's heart was beating fast, but he was otherwise fine.

Travis, however, was not fine. Not fine at all. He could have hurt his dog. All because he hadn't been thinking.

He hadn't been paying attention.

He was so goddamn distracted by the mess that was in his head and his heart that he hadn't followed the simplest rules of the road. He heard the familiar sound of a siren, then a few seconds later there was a knock on his window. He rolled it down.

"Hey, Johnny," he said to the cop he knew well.

"Hey, Trav. I know you weren't drinking and driving. At least you better not have been."

"No sir," he said, shaking his head.

"What got into you then, running a light?"

That was a good question. Travis had never so much as had a ticket before. He never sped. He was careful behind the wheel at all times. He glanced at his dog. He thought of his talk with his mom. What *had* gotten into him?

That's when all the colliding thoughts, all the supposedly foreign feelings, untangled themselves from each other. All the threads, all the knots, all the messy snarl of emotions— they crystallized into something clear. The strange notions that had been rattling around in his brain for last few weeks took hold in his heart, and he was left with one feeling—he missed her.

He knew the answer to Johnny's question. The answer was in the way he felt when he was with Cara.

"A woman," he said, with certainty in his tone. "I was thinking about a woman, and I have no clue what to do about her or how to get her back."

Johnny smiled and nodded. "Know the feeling well. You be more careful next time, you hear?"

"I will," he said, and it occurred to him that Johnny's warning applied both to how he drove and to how he'd treated Cara's heart.

When he arrived home, he grabbed a beer and flopped down on the couch with his dog. "What are we going to do now?"

Henry didn't have an answer either.

As Travis fell asleep later, he wondered if Cara hogged the sheets, and what it was going to take for him to find out.

Chapter Twenty-Five

It was like a hangover, but worse.

Because this awful empty ache wouldn't go away with coffee, eggs, aspirin, or any of the other tricks. Time was the only cure for this stupid heartbreak, and she was looking at a whole awful lot of seconds, minutes, and hours to get rid of the way she felt for that man.

As she rode faster on the elliptical the next morning, she reasoned that he'd made the task of getting over him a bit easier by acting like such an ass. She scoffed out loud as she recalled the things he'd said in the reception room. Mario Batali waxed on about gnocchi on her TV, as she replayed the way Travis tried to dismiss her. Faster, and faster still she pedaled, as if she could burn him off the way she burned off calories.

The TV show switched to a commercial break. A mattress salesperson appeared on the screen, screaming about the deal he had in his store today.

"This day only!"

The date blared across the TV.

She slammed on the pedals, stopping. Breathing hard. She dropped her head to the handles of the elliptical machine. Today was that stupid fireman's auction. She had promised to be there with him, helping in the wings with Henry. The image of the sweet dog loosened the knot of anger she'd been nursing all morning. She had trained that dog; she wanted to see him perform. She longed for that moment of pride. She raised her head and gripped the handlebars hard, digging in with her fingers, sending all her frustration into the machine.

She wasn't even going to be able to enjoy the crowning moment of her job, because there was no way she was walking into the hotel in San Francisco tonight to see the fireman's auction. To think, she'd mapped out the perfect plan to bid on him and take him off the market, to win him no matter what, and, in return, he had so callously ditched her feelings.

She flipped to the TV menu, hoping there would be a comedy, maybe even a spy flick on tonight. Something, anything, to take her mind off where she would have been.

• • •

As he jogged home after an early morning workout at the gym, his phone buzzed with a text message.

He peered at the screen in his hand as his feet pounded along the sidewalk near his house. The message was from Hunter and it instructed him to check his email.

He clicked over and scrolled through a few messages,

but he didn't see the man's name in his inbox. Instead, he spotted an email from the Families of Fallen Firefighters.

Shit. The tension shot sky high in his chest. He feared another note about lack of funds, another plea for help that would go unanswered. He slowed his pace to a walk, took a steadying breath, and read the note.

> *"A donation of $5000 in your name has been made for a job well done. In addition, a matching donation of $5000 has been made from one of our corporate sponsors. This is a HUGE help in restoring some of the services that our communities have come to rely on, including the one-to-one support we provide families. We are so grateful to you and Hunter, and we will be able to reinstate some of our services immediately."*

He stopped in his tracks.

His jaw fell open. He was sure it clanged loudly on the sidewalk.

He rubbed his eyes, blinked, and read the email again to be certain. The sun blared brightly this morning. Maybe it was playing tricks on his eyes. He peered more closely at the screen. The words were there. The donation was real. Hunter had helped the cause.

That ball of stress in his gut unwound. He felt lighter, freer. While the charity's future may not have been *his* burden, he was so damn glad that the organization that had helped his mom to recover could keep doing the good work.

He dialed his biggest client. "That was awfully nice of you. And well beyond the call of duty. To what do I owe the honor?"

"Hey!" Hunter sounded particularly upbeat this morning. "Good to hear from you."

"Even better to hear from you. Or, I should say, to hear from the Families of Fallen Firefighters. You did an amazing thing, man. You helped out in a big way where it's needed most."

Hunter made a *pshaw* sound as if it were nothing. "Just doing my small part. Least I could do after you came through for me yesterday."

"I assume this means you followed my advice and took home a tidy sum," Travis said, resuming his pace.

"Nope. I lost even more money after you left," Hunter said, sounding oddly jubilant—the complete opposite of how he sounded yesterday.

Travis furrowed his brow as he crossed the street to his block. "You hate losing money. Explain."

"Correction. I don't hate losing money. That's what I realized when you left. I actually like making big bets. I love taking risks. That's why I play poker and that's why I do what I do for a living. But the thing is, I was playing poker like it's my job and it's not. I don't want to play the same way I work, and I wasn't having fun when I was trying to be all controlled and methodical."

"But that's what you wanted me to teach you. That's why you came to me," Travis said, the sun blazing at him as it rose higher in the morning sky. "So help me out, since you've thoroughly confused me."

"I did want you to teach me how to play better. How to analyze the risks, study the hands, play like a pro. I hired you because I *thought* I wanted to be some master of the game, and to play like I invest. But then the game became another job. I get enough frustrations at work. I want to play for fun, I want to play without a plan, and sometimes that means I'll lose a lot of money, and sometimes I'll win, and sometimes I'll break even."

"Hey, I'm glad you're happy, though I have no idea what I did to get you there."

"If you hadn't talked frankly to me I wouldn't have been able to see that I needed to do the opposite. You said you'd be happy when I no longer needed you. And I don't need you anymore, because now I'm just playing to have fun. So in a roundabout way, your final kick in the pants was exactly what I needed, and that's why I wanted to thank you."

"And fire me, too," Travis said with a laugh, as he reached his porch and took out his key.

"I hope you're cool with it."

"I couldn't be happier that you no longer need me. And thank you for the donation. You didn't need to do that, but I appreciate it," he said. "And it sounds like you're going to have a blast playing cards without a plan."

"I am," Hunter said, and they said good-bye as Travis walked inside his home.

Henry ran to greet him. As Travis refilled the dog's water bowl, he scratched Henry between the ears. "Buddy, we've got a lot of work to do. You know that?"

Henry raised an ear as if he were listening.

"Somebody just did something special for us. So now it's our turn," he said, then stood up. But really, it was *his* turn. Hunter had given him a beautiful gift. Like a fairy god-mother in the stories Travis had read to Megan when he was younger, the man had swooped in to save the day. With his big *thank you*, Hunter had freed Travis from the weight of needing to be the hero for an organization.

The pressure Travis now felt came from someplace else. From a place inside him he'd tried hard to deny existed. But it had insisted on being heard anyway.

That meant something else was at stake tonight.

Something he hadn't expected to want. But he wanted it now. So much that he couldn't imagine living without it.

Or really, living without her.

But after what he'd said to Cara last night, he knew he needed to do something as meaningful for her as Hunter had done for him.

He called Becker. Sure, there was a part of him that could see the value in operating without a playbook. But winging it would not work now.. He needed his men to help him win one woman tonight.

Especially since he had a sinking feeling that the one woman was incredibly pissed at him.

. . .

Becker parked his hands behind his head, tipped back in the chair in his kitchen, and laughed. Loudly. Knowingly. Enjoying every single second of Travis's big ask.

Travis rolled his eyes. "So will you help me?"

Becker held up his hand. "Just tell me again when it was you realized you were a complete and utter dipshit? 'Cause that's my favorite part of the story."

Megan chimed in, drumming her fingers on the table. "Yeah. Mine, too. Was it when Mom gave you a talking to or was it when Mr. Safety ran the light? Or was it, wait, don't tell me, was it the look on Cara's face when she drove away from you last night?"

Travis motioned with his fingers for them to keep piling on. "I deserve it. I know. Just keep 'em coming."

"Seriously," Megan said with a laugh as she took a drink from her iced tea. "You are a piece of work. I knew you were in love with her, and I knew she was in love with you. And you fucked up."

"No. Kidding." Travis exaggerated the words. "I am well aware of that."

"Just tell me one last time," Becker said. "Tell me the moment when you, the avowed single man who swore he'd never get involved with any woman, who was so firmly against commitment that he once tried to keep me away from the woman who became the love of my life," he said, stopping to reach for Megan's hand and hold it tightly. "Tell me when you knew you'd been in love with Cara for the last ten years and then some."

Travis gulped and took a deep breath. "Look. It is what it is. Okay? Now, I just need your help."

"No," Becker said firmly, slapping his free hand on the table. "Tell me."

Megan dropped her chin into her hand and batted her eyes. "We want to know. C'mon, Travis. You'd do anything for your little sister. Tell me the moment when the most stubborn person I've ever known knew he was wrong."

He heaved a long, frustrated sigh. But he was only frustrated because the clock was ticking. Even though he was throwing caution to the wind, he still needed to line up all the pieces for tonight. "I knew it when I was driving home last night. It all became clear. And then I got home, and I missed her. But if you really want the full story, there were probably a million moments when I felt it and just hadn't realized it. When I brought her the flowers. When I fixed her car and found myself wanting to help out with anything else she'd ever need me to do. Or when she gave me a haircut, and I could see her doing it again and again, every time I needed one. Or when I saw her at Smith's wedding, and my heart started pounding just from looking at her," he said, recounting some of the moments that had read like Latin in his mind at the time, but had now been properly translated to spell out the depths of his feelings. Of course, there were other times, too. Ones just between him and Cara, like in the shower the other day when he'd washed her hair. Or right before then, in her bed, when sex had felt like love for the first time. "I can tell you all that, or I can tell her tonight. Will you just help me?"

Becker nodded and extended a hand. "I always help my men."

Megan stood up and planted a quick kiss on Travis's forehead. "Of course. Though I think I need to call in reinforcements if we're going to convince Cara to show up. She's not too fond of you right now."

. . .

She'd lasted another few hours of this awful day. She was ready to check each one off on her calendar. When she'd made it through the first full twenty-four hours, she'd feel like some real progress had been made. She had mapped out her evening. An hour at the dog park with Violet, then she'd pay a visit to Stacy, then she'd make spicy linguini.

As the afternoon rolled on and she jotted down her list of ingredients, her bell rang, and she opened the door to find Megan and Stacy on her porch. "I don't recall starting a midwife's practice, so do tell me why the two pregnant ladies are at my door."

Stacy laughed. "Let us in."

"Like I have a choice," Cara said, as she gestured for them to come inside.

Stacy pointed to the red couch in her living room. "Sit with us."

"Okay," Cara said, and did as instructed. Perhaps it was the older sister tone of voice that made her obey, and she parked herself between the two women.

"Listen," Stacy said, placing her hand on Cara's leg. "I think you need to go to the auction tonight."

She shook her head adamantly. "No. No. No. And in case that wasn't clear, no."

Megan spoke up. "I know you were planning on going and bidding for him, and I even encouraged you to do so. And I feel terrible because my brother was an ass, but I think you should go."

"Why?" Cara asked, holding her hands out wide. "None of you ladies are telling me why I should go? I put my heart on the line last night, and he just completely dismissed me." Her voice broke, and all the tears that she had shed alone last night came roaring back. Torrential rains poured down her cheeks, and she let the waterworks fly. "It hurt so much."

Her chest ached with the pain. The cruel memory of the way he'd ditched her—*we had a good time*—sliced into her heart once again. Megan leaned across the coffee table to grab some tissues and handed them to Cara.

She dabbed at her cheeks.

Stacy wrapped an arm around her. "Sweetie. I hate seeing you hurt," she said softly, squeezing her shoulder. "More than anything in the world. And I would go to the mats for you, and hurt anyone who hurt you. And in case you haven't noticed, I'm not at Travis's house right now beating him up, even though I could." Stacy held up her fists in the *put up your dukes* pose. Cara managed a small, faint laugh. "So all I'm saying is, trust me. I know that's hard, but I don't think you'll regret going. I'll be by your side. And if you want to leave, we will leave. But you trained that dog—"

"Do you mean Travis? Because dog is a nice word, and I don't think he was so nice."

"She means Henry," Megan said, and for some reason the fact that Travis's sister was here made her consider the request more seriously.

"I *do* want to see Henry," Cara said under her breath.

"You can't let this change you," Stacy said. "You hold your head up high and you go. You have every right to be there tonight to cheer on the dog."

"You want to go, don't you?" Megan asked. Cara nodded and squeaked out a yes. "Then let's get you ready, and we'll take you, and you can see the dog do his thing."

"Promise me you'll stay with me the whole time, Stace?"

Stacy crossed her heart. "Promise," she said.

Chapter Twenty-Six

No fucking way.

Was the guy from Santa Barbara doing a full-on strip tease?

He was gyrating. He was grinding. He was getting the ladies all worked up.

Travis hit his palm against his forehead from backstage at the ballroom of the hotel in San Francisco hosting the California Bachelor Fireman's Auction. Damn, he was glad he wasn't gunning for victory anyway, because this was not going to be an easy one tonight with that tough act to follow.

Travis peered around the heavy red velvet curtain to see the bleached blond emcee hooting and hollering as the firefighter on stage tossed his T-shirt into the audience then teased them by undoing the top snap on his pants. The crowd, mostly women, cheered and clapped.

The man was going to clean up big time. He stroked his thumbs along the suspenders, as if he were going to take those off too. Then he turned around, and smacked his own ass, then did the back-it-up move.

The emcee wiped her hand across her brow and brought the mic to her lips. "Whew. Is it hot in here or what? Let's give it up for Mike McNulty from Santa Barbara. I might even need to see what I brought in my wallet, because I'd like to take that home," she said, and pointed to Mike, who preened once more for the audience as he pretended he was about to unzip his pants.

Travis glanced at his dog, who waited dutifully by his feet. His sister was by his side; she'd keep an eye on the pooch once Travis was introduced. Nothing mattered to him but Cara, and he'd caught a brief glimpse of her earlier in the back row, next to her sister. She'd kept her head down, but he'd spotted her right away, those red streaks in her hair visible from across the crowd. She didn't need colorful highlights for him to find her. He could find her anywhere because she was all he saw. She was all he'd ever wanted to see, and he was amazed at how stupid he'd been to miss what was right under his nose all along.

After several minutes of heated bidding, a tattooed brunette in the front row bid eight hundred dollars and won rights to take Mike McNulty home for the evening.

"And now, we have our second to last man of the night. Hailing from the Hidden Oaks fire department—" The blonde stopped and held up a hand. "Wait. Hidden Oaks. As in home of the bestselling calendar with the hottest men in all the country? Oh fan me now, ladies. Fan me now."

The blonde pretended she was about to faint, and the crowd laughed. "I hear the pickings are getting slimmer up there though. The men of Hidden Oaks have been falling like flies. Evidently, something is in the water in that town because the star of the calendar just got married yesterday."

The crowd booed.

"I know. Can you believe it? And I hear the fire chief is off the market too. Some lucky lady nabbed him last year, and he'll be saying 'I do' any day."

Another round of sad boos. Megan pretended to hiss at the audience. Travis patted her back. "They're all jealous of you," he whispered.

"But have no fear," the emcee said, returning to a perky voice as she urged the crowd to cheer. "Because there are still plenty of single, bachelor firemen in Hidden Oaks, and we have a top-notch competitor here tonight. Allow me to bring out one of California's finest volunteer firemen, Travis Jansen from Hidden Oaks."

Travis strutted onstage and shot the crowd his best sexy, seductive smile. The women cheered, but the smile was for one woman. The one in the back row who wouldn't look at him. He didn't let that deter him though. He was on a mission to prove himself to her.

"Travis turns thirty this summer, he's been with the department for nine years, and he's a professional poker player on the side," the emcee said, reading off the card as she recited Travis's "measurements" like he was a contestant in a beauty pageant. He parked his hands on his hips. He wore his turnouts, as most of the contestants did, because looking the part was vital, and that included the goods under the shirt.

"How about it? Can we see what's underneath that T-shirt?" she said.

"Absolutely," he said, quickly complying with the request as he stripped off his blue T-shirt and tossed it to the audience.

Cheers greeted him, and he wished that Cara were one of the women making some noise. But as his eyes roamed the room, he saw she wasn't. She kept her arms crossed over her chest and her lips fixed in a straight line.

"Travis enjoys football, laughing, the company of a good woman, and his dog. Oh," the emcee said, as if she'd discovered something delicious. "Who doesn't love a dog!" She turned to Travis. "And I hear you might even have brought this dog with you tonight."

"I did. Would you like to meet my puppy?"

"A puppy!" The emcee cheered, then egged on the crowd. "I do, I do, I do. I might even have to bid on you, too."

Travis turned to lock eyes with Megan off stage, then his little dog. "C'mere, Henry."

That was all the canine needed to hear. He knew his commands, and he followed them to the letter. The dog ran across the stage, doing the one thing Cara had trained him to do.

Perfectly.

Like a champion.

He wasn't distracted by the emcee oohing and ahhing. He didn't get scared by the crowds. He didn't let the noise frighten him away. He trotted, and when he reached him, Travis gave the command for the special trick they'd planned.

Travis patted his chest. "Jump."

On cue, Henry leapt high in the air. Travis held out his arms and caught the dog, bringing him close to his chest. He turned to the audience, who cheered for the fireman and his dog. Just as he had hoped. Even Cara had a smile on her beautiful face.

"Let the bidding begin for man and dog. What do we have?"

A brunette in a slinky dress raised her hand and offered five hundred dollars.

But then, Smith stood up. He raised his hand. "One thousand."

The emcee startled, surprised to hear a masculine voice bidding on Travis. She quickly composed herself. "Okay, we've got one thousand from the gentleman over there. Anyone else?"

Jackson stood up. "Two thousand," he shouted above the crowd.

"And we have two thousand," the emcee said, pointing to Travis's other buddy from the department.

A redhead in jeans and a tight top shot her hand in the air. "I'd like to bid twenty-one hundred. But do I even have the right equipment?" She pointed to her breasts, and the women around her laughed.

The emcee flashed a wide smile to the woman. "Now, now. We don't issue any rules for our contestants on likes and dislikes. Any bachelor fireman is free to get on stage. It's all the buyer's risk. Are you bidding, sweetheart?"

The redhead nodded. "I'll take my chances. I like the looks of him without his shirt on. I'd like to check out his hose."

Travis reined in a smirk. He'd heard that line before. They all had.

"And we have twenty-one hundred. Anyone else?" the emcee asked.

Becker rose. "Three thousand. Let's take this man off the market."

The emcee blinked and nearly stuttered as she spoke. "Three thousand. Wow. That is our highest bid so far."

"I can go higher," Becker offered, and Travis laughed. Because Becker was playing with the house's money—Travis's money, to be precise. He had dipped into his savings, liquidating plenty of it. Which meant he'd be operating without much of a safety net. He was taking a risk without any assurances. But that's what made certain risks worthwhile—the reward. He had no guarantee, but Cara was worth taking a chance for. She was the best reward there could ever be.

"Um," the emcee said, clearly thrown by the odd turn of events. "Does anyone else want to bid on Travis Jansen?"

There were whispers in the crowd, but Travis doubted anyone was trying to beat Becker's number. It was simply too high. That was the point.

"Look. He's just not available. If I have to bid more, I will," Becker said, his deep voice booming across the room.

Travis locked eyes with Cara in the back of the ballroom and she seemed as surprised as the emcee. With Henry in his arms, Travis reached for the mic. "May I?" he whispered to the blonde.

"Have at it," she said.

He took the mic, and even though he'd practiced what to say and rehearsed the words in front of his mirror, he was still flying solo right now. Because he was about to do the one thing he swore he'd never do. Put his heart on the line. A flurry of nerves skittered through his body, and he had no choice but to ignore them.

"The man's right. I'm off the market. Or at least, I'd very much like to be. Because there's a woman who has my heart, only she doesn't know it yet. So tonight, I am telling her. I want her to know that I don't want anyone else bidding on me. I won't take a chance of going home with anyone but her, so I asked my buddies to take me out of the running. Because I am out of the running as far as I'm concerned." He kept his gaze focused on Cara, even across the throngs of people stuffed into the raucous ballroom. "I've been out of the running for a long, long time. The problem is, it took me losing her to realize that I needed her. And that I was in love with her," he said, and there were no more nerves. They were all gone. Because no matter what she said, no matter how she responded, he simply had to tell her. He had to give her his heart, because no one else could possibly ever have it. "She went out on a limb for me, so I'm going out on a limb for her right here. And I'm hoping that she still feels the same, and that she'll have me."

He walked down the three steps from the stage and cut through the crowd, his heart beating faster and faster still when Cara met his eyes. A tear streaked down her cheek as he neared her. The other women in the crowd placed their hands on their hearts, cheering him on as he crossed the distance to the woman he'd fallen in love with. When he reached her, he stood before her and brushed his free hand over her cheek. She trembled and couldn't contain a smile.

"I couldn't get you out of my system either, because you've always been here," he said, tapping his chest, right next to where he held the small dog. "I just didn't know it, because I've never been in love before. I had no clue what I was feeling because it was so foreign and so unusual and something I vowed I didn't want. But the truth is, I was feeling it all along for you. I always have. And I'm truly sorry for the completely stupid things I said last night. I want to go all in with you. Only you, always you, if you'll have me."

She didn't answer immediately. She raised her chin high and crossed her arms. His heart plummeted as she seemed to close herself off. But her eyes were lit up and sparkling, so he held on to a kernel of hope that he hadn't lost her.

"Are you sure?" Her voice was soft and just for him.

He furrowed his brow. "Am I sure?"

She nodded. "Yes. I want to know if you're certain. I want to know if you're going to freak out again over doing something like this. Like having a relationship."

"Cara, I can't imagine living without you. I don't ever want to lose you again."

"So you're in it for good now?"

He nodded vigorously. She was putting him through his paces, and he was more than willing to be tested. "I'm crazy for you and always have been. But more than that, I am madly in love with you and can't stand the thought of not having you by my side."

"You just want my eggplant Parmesan, don't you?" she said, her lips curving up in a wild grin.

He laughed as that kernel of hope expanded. "I do, but not as much as I want you."

"You can have both," she said, her eyes shining brightly as she uncrossed her arms and stepped closer.

"Good. Now, can I kiss you in front of everyone so that it's all official that I'm not a bachelor fireman anymore?"

"You are so not a bachelor fireman," she said, grabbing the waistband of his pants and tugging him close. Possessively. "You are all mine."

"That's all I want to be."

Then he kissed her.

"I was right, ladies and gentlemen. There's something in the water in Hidden Oaks," the emcee said. "I'm moving there, and I'll be picking through whoever remains at that department, because it seems that there's one less bachelor fireman in that town."

When Travis broke the kiss, he took Cara's hand and walked out the door with his woman and his dog.

Epilogue

Cara returned to Hidden Oaks after a training lesson with
a new client. A couple from New York was spending some
time in the Bay Area after the birth of their first child, and
they had wanted some extra sessions for their dog. They
were full of so much affection for each other, the dog, and
their new baby daughter that it had warmed Cara's heart to
spend an hour with them.

She'd be seeing them again in another week to work on
some more skills. Helping dogs adjust to no longer being
the baby of the family was part of her repertoire. Maybe
someday, she'd help Violet and Henry with those skills. She'd
already taught Henry to stop barking when Travis spanked
her, so she was confident she could handle any curveball
a dog threw her way. For now, she was simply happy to be
heading home to see her man and cook him a good meal.

She pulled into the driveway of Travis's home, next to his truck. She'd moved in with him last month, since her lease was up and it made sense. After all, they'd been spending every night together. Every day, too, when they weren't working.

She cut the engine, grabbed the bag of groceries from the passenger seat, and unlocked the front door. "I'm making your favorite pasta primavera tonight," she called out, as she headed up the steps and into the kitchen. "You know I love cooking for you."

But the kitchen was empty. Travis didn't answer her. None of the dogs greeted her either. Weird. He must be out walking them.

She set to work emptying the bag on the counter and planning what spices she'd need, when a rap on the kitchen window startled her. She nearly jumped, but then smiled when she saw Travis on the back deck, knocking on the window-pane. "Come outside," he mouthed.

She headed to the sliding glass door and stepped onto the deck. Both dogs raced over to greet her.

"Sit," she told them. They did as asked and she rewarded them with pats on the head. Then Travis got his reward, too, in a long, lingering kiss. He tugged her close, wrapping his arms around her. They kissed every time one of them came home for the day. This was everything she'd ever wanted. The home, the dogs, and the mad, wild, crazy heart-pounding love.

"Hey," he said when he broke the kiss. "I taught Henry a new trick. Want to see?"

"Of course."

Travis called Henry to him, and then knelt and began

fiddling with the dog's collar.

"What are you doing?" she asked, trying to figure out what he was up to. He seemed to be reaching inside something that looked awfully familiar, almost as if Henry was wearing a small leather pouch. As Travis switched to one knee, Cara gasped.

Henry *was* wearing a pouch, and Travis was dipping his hand inside it. "He's been holding onto this for me," Travis said, and her heart beat furiously, speeding up to a highway robbery pace as hope dashed and darted all through her bloodstream.

He looked up at her, holding a gorgeous diamond ring in his palm. "Cara Bailey, I am so in love with you, and I can't bear the thought of you ever slipping away from me. I love you and I love our blended family," he said, gesturing to the two dogs and making her laugh with his remark. "And I can't let another day go by without asking you to be my wife. Will you marry me?"

"You bet I will," she said, kneeling down on the wooden deck to join him as he slid the ring onto her finger. Then she threw her arms around him and kissed him. "Why don't we elope? We could even catch a flight to Vegas tomorrow."

"You're on. I'll see your tomorrow, and I'll raise it to tonight," he said. "Let's head to the airport."

That sounded damn good to her, too.

Acknowledgments

Thank you to all who made this book possible. To Stacy and Alycia, who helped me find the right path to Cara and Travis' romance, to Michelle for her passion for all my books, and to Kelly, who stands by my side every day! I am grateful for the dedication of all at Entangled who have helped make this series a success, from Heather and Heather, to Jessica, to Katie, to Curtis, to Liz and many more. Thank you to Tanya Farrell, who read an early draft and to Kim Bias, who read the final draft. Thank you to all the passionate bloggers and readers who embrace sexy romance. Thank you to my family for supporting my imaginary worlds. Most of all, thank you so very much to the people who make my dreams possible every day – my readers. You are the bomb.

And thank you, as always, to my dogs. My daily companions!

About the Author

Lauren Blakely writes sexy contemporary romance novels with heat, heart, and humor, and many of her titles have appeared on both the *New York Times* bestseller list and the *USA Today* bestseller list. Like the heroine in her novel *Far Too Tempting*, she thinks life should be filled with family, laughter, and the kind of love that love songs promise. Lauren lives in California with her husband, children, and dogs. She loves hearing from readers! Her bestselling series include Caught Up in Love, Seductive Nights, No Regrets, and Fighting Fire. She is also releasing a new series called Sinful Nights, which fans of Seductive Nights and her fireman books will love! Lauren writes for young adults under the name Daisy Whitney. To receive an email when Lauren releases a new book, text BLAKELY + your email address to 678-249-3375 (please use the actual + sign)

Discover the **Fighting Fire** *series...*

Burn for Me

Jamie Lansing has had it bad for firefighter Smith Grayson for as long as they've been friends. Yes, he's ridiculously charming and she might stare a little too long at his abs, but his dirty-talking, rough-around-the-edges ways aren't for her. But Smith has only ever had eyes for Jamie. When she suggests a week of no-strings-attached sex to get him out of her system, Smith knows this is his one chance to prove he's not just the man she needs in her bed, but the man she needs in her life.

Melt for Him

Also by Lauren Blakely

Far Too Tempting

9/15

CPSIA information can be obtained at www.ICGtesting.com
Printed in the USA
LVOW11s1543140915

454091LV00001B/34/P

9 781943 892136